LOUISE'S CROSSING

Sarah R. Shaber

Severn House Large Print
London & New York

This first large print edition published 2019
in Great Britain and the USA by
SEVERN HOUSE PUBLISHERS LTD of
Eardley House, 4 Uxbridge Street, London W8 7SY.
First world regular print edition published 2019 by
Severn House Publishers Ltd.

British Library Cataloguing in Publication Data
A CIP catalogue record for this title is available from the British Library.

ISBN-13: 9780727892348

Severn House Publishers support the Forest Stewardship Council™
[FSC™], the leading international forest certification organisation. All
our titles that are printed on FSC certified paper carry the FSC logo.

Typeset by Palimpsest Book Production Ltd.,
Falkirk, Stirlingshire, Scotland.
Printed and bound in Great Britain by
T J International, Padstow, Cornwall.

For my awesome mother,
Frances Purvis Rock

Acknowledgments

I owe special thanks to my friend Linna Barnes, who gave me a copy of her mother's diary, written in February of 1943 and November of 1944. Mary Jane Barnes' diary was a gold mine. It described Ms Barnes' crossing of the Atlantic Ocean to take up a job at OSS London, and later her experience of living in the UK during World War II. I've used her first-hand account as a source for a number of scenes in *Louise's Crossing*. You'll find a biography of Mary Jane Mulford Barnes at the end of this book in the Author's Note.

I must also thank Ben Steelman, David Munger, Tony Burton and James Benn for explaining the properties of torpedoes and grenades, and for answering other questions about World War II warships and such.

As always, the support of my family: my husband Steve, our son Sam, our daughter and son-in-law Katie and Matt Lindsay, have been critical to keeping me writing. Our grandsons Brandon and Nathan are a bonus!

I cannot imagine my life, writing or otherwise, without my writing buddies, Margaret Maron, Diane Chamberlain, Katy Munger, Alex Sokoloff, Kathy Trochek and Bren Witchger. Or without my friend and agent Vicky Bijur.

I am especially thankful that Severn House, now led by Kate Lyall Grant, offered to publish the first Louise Pearlie mystery during the Great Recession of 2008, when contracts were as scarce as hen's teeth.

I am so fortunate that Quail Ridge Books in Raleigh is my home bookstore.

One

Washington, DC
February 6, 1944

On my way to work I stopped to watch the man and boy play. The day was as frigid as all the days in February had been, but the sun was out and the man had broken a big hole in the ice of the Reflecting Pool so he and the boy could play with a toy boat. The man had taken off his gloves to wind it up. It was a Liberty ship; I could tell by its silhouette. The boy, who was wearing a sailor's cap and looked to be about four years old, was so excited he was jumping up and down in anticipation.

'OK,' the man said, handing the boat to the boy. 'Put it gently in the water, then turn the switch on.'

The boy took the boat and set it carefully in the pool and flipped the 'on' switch. The boat took off valiantly across the pool, phony smoke rising from its stack, the tiny motor making a satisfying chugging noise. The little boy shrieked with excitement, and I felt like doing the same thing. I'd be crossing the ocean in a Liberty ship myself soon. Ever since I'd gotten my new assignment, I'd catch my heart beating erratically, or my breath coming shallowly and quickly, or a headache developing in my temples. I was thrilled, but I couldn't tell anyone outside the

1

office where I was headed. After all, I still worked for the Office of Strategic Services and I had to keep my mouth shut.

I watched the man and boy enjoying the toy boat's voyage. Then it all went wrong.

The little boat hit a chunk of ice, spun about and hit another, then tipped over, sinking, leaving just a few bubbles on the surface of the pool. The child burst into tears.

'Don't worry,' the father said to his son. 'These things can happen on a sea voyage. Sailors have to be very brave.' The boy nodded, wiping his eyes with his gloved hands.

I went up to them. 'Can I help?' I said. 'I could find a long stick or something.'

The man grinned at me. 'I came prepared,' he said. Rolling up his pants legs, he revealed a tall pair of Wellington boots. He climbed over the edge of the pool and waded out to the last known location of USS *Toy Boat*, took off his gloves, rolled up his sleeves and felt around under the water, bringing up the dripping boat. Back on shore, his son wrapped his arms around his father's legs. 'Let's go home, sailor,' the man said. 'You can help me take the boat apart and we'll dry it out. It'll be fine, I bet.' I watched the two of them go off hand in hand, the little boy taking three steps to each one of his father's.

The episode unnerved me. If my own ship had trouble on the ocean, no giant man in wellies would appear to lift it out of danger. Since the Nazi submarine wolf packs had retreated, the Atlantic wasn't as dangerous as it once was, but there were still lone wolves prowling about, fierce winter storms, and as any ship drew closer to land, Axis airplanes determined to sink any Allied cargo ships they could.

When I got to work, I relaxed a bit since everyone there knew where I'd been reassigned, so it was no secret. That had its drawbacks, though, as I became the butt of every British joke in the OSS joke book. As I walked through the artists' work-room, one of the guys looked up at me, smiling. I waited for the expected ribbing. 'I hope you like boiled mutton,' he said. 'That's all those Limeys ever eat.'

'And don't forget the potato sandwiches,' one of the others piped in. 'Cold potato sandwiches. With Marmite gluing it all together.'

'Don't you worry about me,' I answered. 'I'm packing plenty of Spam and peanut butter.'

No sooner had I gotten into my drafty office and hung up my coat and hat than Merle came in with a cup of hot coffee and a strawberry-jam-filled biscuit for me. Merle heaved himself up on my desk, dangling his cowboy boot-shod feet. Merle was a Texan through and through. He'd been a newspaper artist before the war, but now he was one of our best forgers.

My office was clean and tidy, ready for its next occupant, except for the shoebox that held the few personal things I could take with me. It was already taped shut.

'This your last day?' he asked, noticing the box.

'Yes,' I answered. 'But please, please don't tell anyone else. I don't want a lot of fuss. I'm leaving

3

as soon as I get my last briefing from Miss Osborne. I should sail a few days from now; I don't know when exactly yet.'

'How far can you swim under a field of burning oil?' he asked, winking at me as he slid off my desk.

'Very funny,' I said.

He reached out to shake my hand. 'In case I don't see you again before you leave.' He didn't let go of my hand, but leaned forward and kissed my forehead. 'Be careful.'

'I will, I promise.'

'Write us occasionally.'

'I will.'

After Merle left, I glanced around my office to see what else needed to be done, but even my inbox was empty. I felt as if my life in DC was already over.

Miss Osborne, whom I admired as much as any person I had met in Washington, went over a checklist with me.

'You have your passport and your AGO card?' The Adjutant General's Office card identified me as a member of the United States military. As such, I couldn't be tortured if I was captured. Supposedly.

'Yes, ma'am.'

'I'll call you with your orders a day before its time to leave. It shouldn't be more than a few days from now. Your ship will be carrying a mixed cargo but also a number of "casual passengers" such as yourself, going to the United Kingdom for various reasons. You don't have a specific cover; use your real name and associate with the passengers as you naturally would. You're just a file clerk and a former supervisor of yours now stationed in London has requested you for his office typing pool, that's all. But I don't have to tell you how to handle yourself.' Then she looked up from her list and smiled at me. 'I wish I wasn't losing you,' she said. 'But with invasion imminent, our Morale Operations station in London will become the front line of this branch.'

The London office of the Office of Strategic Services, the United States' espionage agency, was located smack in the middle of London, at 70 Grosvenor Square, quite close to the US Embassy. Colonel David K.E. Bruce, scion of a wealthy Maryland family, was its Director. With an invasion of Europe imminent, every branch of OSS in DC was now represented in its London office. My office, the Morale Operations Unit, was responsible for what we called 'black propaganda' – that is, outright lies and misinformation distributed to the German people.

I struggled to express myself adequately. 'Alice,' I said, using her given name. 'Thank you for everything. For recommending me. And for allowing me to go.'

'You always seemed to me to be a woman in search of adventure. London is not the happiest place to be these days, but there will still be plenty for you to do, at work and at play. Oh, and here.' She rummaged in the papers stacked on her desk and handed me one with several names and addresses on them. 'Don't be shy

– contact these people. They are friends of mine; they'll show you around and they know not to ask questions.'

She pulled a square tin out of her desk and handed it over to me. It was a box of airmail stationery, with square envelopes and onionskin paper. 'Write occasionally, OK?' she said.

'Of course.' It looked as if I was going to spend most of my free time writing letters home.

Even she couldn't resist a final quip. 'I hope you know how to row a lifeboat,' she said, grinning at me.

I went straight back to my office, grabbed my shoebox and slinked out a side door during the afternoon coffee break without giving anyone a chance to make a fuss.

I contemplated my packing. I'd been working on it forever, it seemed. I was permitted to take a footlocker, a large suitcase and a musette bag, a small backpack that I could carry over my shoulder. The footlocker would be stored in the hold where I couldn't reach it during the voyage, so I needed to make sure all my essentials were in the two other cases. I'd requisitioned the footlocker already, and Phoebe led me to the attic where she offered the largest suitcase I thought I could carry on my own from her worn set of navy-blue leather Lady Baltimore luggage. 'Milt and I went to a lot of swell places before the Depression,' Phoebe said. 'Sometimes I took all seven pieces.'

So now the three pieces of luggage lay open in my bedroom.

I couldn't tell anyone at my boarding house where I was headed, but from what I was packing it would be obvious I wasn't going anywhere comfortable. Some of my footlocker space was reserved for non-perishable food. Mostly jars of peanut butter, cans of Spam and Vienna sausages. Without any guilt at all, I'd bought two pounds of sugar and some coffee on the black market. I'd been advised to pack several packages of sanitary napkins and rolls of toilet paper. Liquor was terribly expensive in London, but alcohol couldn't be transported in the hold, so I unhappily settled on one bottle of Gordon's gin, which I'd carry in my musette bag. I had no room for vermouth. After this bottle was empty, I supposed I'd have to learn to drink warm beer.

I'd requisitioned an arctic parka, lined boots, heavy gloves and thick socks, and to my surprise had received them in the correct sizes. I cushioned the contents of my footlocker with them. I wouldn't need such heavy clothing on board the ship. I included a set of flannel sheets and a blanket in case my future digs were short of linens. My wool coat, one set of long underwear and a pair of flannel pajamas went into my suitcase.

I added a small photo of Joe in a silver frame to the personal items tucked into the musette bag.

A wave of emotion crashed over me and tears started down my face. I sat down on the bed to collect myself. Joe Prager was my lover. He was a Czech refugee with a British passport who had been a boarder here when I arrived. Ostensibly, he taught Slavic languages at Georgetown University, but I discovered that he was working undercover for the JDC, an organization struggling to get Jewish refugees out of Europe. We fell in love and spent time alone together whenever we could. We never discussed marriage. That was impossible. I mean, I didn't know who he really was! He'd been reassigned overseas, and I had no idea where he was stationed or if he would ever return to the United States. I guessed he was in Lisbon, a neutral port, where a JDC operative had been murdered, leaving an opening that needed to be filled.

What if Joe returned to DC while I was overseas? I could hardly bear the thought. I had no reason to think he would, especially as the Allies geared up for an invasion that would displace even more refugees. I knew Joe well enough to be sure that wherever he was he would be focused on the job at hand, not on a future impossible to predict. I had decided to do the same thing. Instead of fretting over him, I would accept the job that was offered me, no matter where it took me. Besides, if Joe did return to DC, he would come straight here, to my boarding house, and Phoebe would be able to give him my APO address to write to me. So I would know if he was safe, and that was all I could hope for.

Phoebe's soft knock sounded at my door. I so hoped she wasn't going to cry again. I didn't think I could bear it. I would miss my life here in my boarding house and my friends, but except for my worry over Joe, I was so excited that I hadn't shed a single tear myself. When I opened my door, I was glad to see that Phoebe was dry-eyed and collected.

8

She glanced over at my packing. 'England,' she said, guessing correctly. Just the word made my heart soar. Never in my wildest dreams had I ever thought I would live and work in Europe. It was Europe in the midst of a terrible war, but still. England! London! Westminster Abbey! Big Ben! None of which I had ever dreamed I would see.

'You know I can't say,' I said, but I was sure my smile betrayed me.

'You really want to go, don't you?' she said.

I admitted that I did.

Phoebe sat on the edge of my bed next to me. 'I just don't understand,' she said. 'It's so dangerous.'

'I'll be fine.' There were bunkers under all the American offices that ringed Grosvenor Square where OSS and the US Embassy could operate for days if they had to. 'Someone has to go,' I continued. 'We have to win this war.' Of course, I didn't mention the invasion which was still secret.

'That we do.' Both of Phoebe's sons had enlisted in the Navy. Milt was back home, missing an arm, but Tom was still stationed in the Pacific.

'I want to give you a little something,' Phoebe said, holding out a tiny package of tissue paper with a thin pink ribbon tied around it.

'But you've given me so much,' I said. 'The necklace, this luggage, and, well' – and here I drew in my breath, feeling sadness for the first time – 'a second home.'

'I don't have a daughter,' Phoebe said. 'So I'd like you to have it.'

I took the tiny package from her and opened

9

it. Like all Phoebe's jewelry, the ring was art deco from the twenties, a tiny diamond surrounded by even smaller blue stones in a square filigree white-gold setting. 'It's not much,' Phoebe said. 'The diamond is real, but those are zircons, not sapphires. You know I had to sell all my good jewels during the Depression. But I hope it reminds you of us.'

The ring was darling. And it matched the lavaliere Phoebe had already given me. I slipped it on my right hand.

'Thank you,' I said.

'Write us,' she said.

'You know I will.'

She left without her usual lecture about what was proper and appropriate for a single woman to do, even in wartime. Thank goodness.

Dellaphine was at her range in the kitchen, hovering over two cast-iron skillets with chicken bubbling in hot lard. I loved her fried chicken. I was pretty sure they didn't fry chicken in England.

'Oh, Dellaphine, thank you for fixing chicken today,' I said. 'I don't know when I'll have it again.'

'Miss Phoebe said to cook your favorite things for Sunday dinner,' Dellaphine said, keeping her back to me as she turned the chicken with her granny fork. 'But why someone who won't even tell her friends when she is leaving them or where she is going should get a special dinner is beyond me.'

Her daughter, Madeleine, looked up from the kitchen table, where she was browsing through

10

the colored newspaper, and said, 'Momma, you know Louise can't tell us where she's headed. It's secret.'

Dellaphine turned away from the range and glared at the two of us, one hand on a hip, brandishing the fork. 'We should let those foreigners fight for theyselves,' she said.

Madeleine just shook her head as she turned the newspaper pages, knowing there was no point in arguing with her mother.

'Once I get to my posting, I can write you, tell you where I am and give you my APO address to write back to me,' I said.

'I ain't got no time to write,' Dellaphine said.

I started to speak, but Madeleine gave me a warning look. Best slink away, I thought, moving toward the door.

'Wait,' Dellaphine said. She turned and picked up a round tin and handed it to me. It had to weigh two pounds. 'I made you some pralines for your trip,' she said. 'They don't melt and keep real well. Don't worry if you start to see little white spots on them after a few weeks. They're still good. That's just the sugar crystallizing.'

For the first time all day I felt a lump in my throat.

'Dellaphine, thank you so much.' It must have taken all our sugar and butter and extra hours in the kitchen for her to make these.

'It was nothing,' she said, turning back to the range, stabbing a chicken breast to turn it. 'Go on and set the table now. And Miss Phoebe say to set out the champagne glasses.'

* * *

11

I found Ada in the dining room throwing one of Phoebe's lace tablecloths over the table. She was better put together than she often was on Sundays, wearing a caftan and matching turban. Ada's gig as a clarinet player in the Willard Hotel band kept her up late most Saturday nights. She smoothed out wrinkles in the tablecloth as I went to the china cabinet to get plates.

'Done packing?' she asked.

'Mostly.'

'I can tell you're excited. Aren't you at all scared?' Ada lived most of her days scared. She was married to a German Luftwaffe pilot who'd left her and returned to Germany when the Nazis took power. She didn't dare try to get a divorce for fear some nosy government bureaucrat would notice the paperwork and send her to a German-American internment camp.

'I should be, I guess,' I said. 'But I'm just not.'

Ada collected silverware from a drawer and followed behind me as I set down the plates.

'February is not a great time to cross the Atlantic,' she said.

'Thousands of people are doing it,' I said.

'Yeah, and hundreds don't make it.' She caught my eye, which I'd been trying to avoid. 'Is it too late to change your mind? You're a civilian. No one can make you go.'

'I want to go.'

'That's just wacky, honey,' she said. 'You can serve your country right here.'

'Someone has to staff our offices overseas.'

'I guess so. You know how much I'll miss you,

12

don't you? Heaven knows who Phoebe will rent your room to next!'

We were unnaturally quiet at dinner. I was the only one who appeared to have an appetite. I greedily worked my way through fried chicken, mashed potatoes and green beans. The green beans were canned, but we'd put them up ourselves with beans from our Victory garden, so they were still darn tasty. No one else – Phoebe, Ada, Milt or Henry – was doing justice to the meal. And they were avoiding meeting my eyes. I didn't know whether to be grateful they were so fond of me or annoyed that they were spoiling what might be my last Sunday dinner with them for a very long time.

Phoebe broke the silence. 'Do your parents know where you're going?' she asked.

'Not exactly, but they know I'm going overseas,' I said. 'But I'll write them just as soon as I can, of course.' I'd gotten leave to spend a long weekend with my family in Wilmington, North Carolina, so I could say goodbye. It was about the longest three days I'd ever experienced. My mother and father were appalled that a single woman would even dream of accepting an assignment that took her across the Atlantic Ocean in February to live in a foreign country for who knew how long. I responded patriotically, reminding them that this was war and young women were being asked to do all sorts of things that would have been unheard of a few years ago. We had to make sacrifices. I didn't remind them that I was thirty years old, had been living for

13

two years in DC by myself and made a salary they wouldn't believe if I told them. And that I was thrilled at the prospect of living in London. I was so relieved to board the train to go back to DC that I went straight to the bar car and ordered a Martini.

'I've got something for you,' Milt said. He pulled an item that clinked out of his pocket and handed it over to me. 'It's my lucky charm,' he said. We had to chuckle, since he'd lost his left arm in a jeep crash on a Pacific Island. 'Hey,' he said, 'it could have been my right arm.'

It was a cheap St Christopher's medal with a four-leaf clover stamped on the other side, threaded through with a chain. It was tarnished and dinged up, maybe from damage that had occurred during Milt's accident.

'My pals gave it to me before I shipped out,' Milt said. 'And I got back home, didn't I?'

'Thanks,' I said, pulling the chain over my head. 'I'll bring it back to you.'

Henry was a middle-aged crusty sort, awfully straight-laced, and I don't think he approved of me or Ada – single women working and doing pretty much what we wanted to. Ada and I thought he had a crush on Phoebe, but as far as we could tell he'd never acted on it. He was sort of a sad sack really.

'I've got a gift for you, too,' Henry said to me, and reached into his pocket. He pulled out two coins that glinted in the candlelight and dropped them into my hand. Two twenty-dollar Liberty Head gold pieces, worth much more than their face value since Roosevelt had taken the country

14

off the gold standard. I hardly knew what to say. I just stared at them, gleaming in my hand. I had no idea what these would be worth on the black market, but it would be plenty.

'Henry,' I said, 'I can't accept these. They're worth too much money.'

Henry shrugged. 'I bought them a long time ago,' he said. 'At face value. Look here,' he said, 'you know I don't approve of you leaving the country; I don't know where you'll be going or what you'll be doing, but it could be dangerous. Gold gets you out of a lot of situations that nothing else will. So carry them with you all the time.'

'Thank you,' I said. 'I will.'

Ada had already given me her gift in the privacy of my bedroom, a set of pink long underwear. 'Just because you need to wear layers of clothes in this weather doesn't mean you can't have feminine unmentionables,' she'd said to me.

Talking openly about my departure seemed to have loosened everyone up. Milt reached for the bowl of mashed potatoes and soon my friends were tucking into their meal with more enthusiasm. Dellaphine brought out one of my favorite desserts: apple pie.

Phoebe served me a large slice. I ate every crumb of it.

'Let's have our champagne in the lounge,' Henry said, 'where the fire is.' We trooped down the hall and settled into our usual seats. Milt stoked the fire while Henry popped the champagne cork and filled our glasses. Phoebe took two glasses into the kitchen for Dellaphine and

Madeleine. I was toasted by all and felt myself blush.

'Please, stop,' I said. 'Enough.'

The telephone rang. Henry went out into the hall to answer it.

Milt made the most of his absence. 'Don't pay attention to Henry,' he said. 'Or' – and here he winked at his mother – 'what other people say. I think it's swell what you're doing. I wish I was shipping out somewhere.' With his one hand, he pulled a cigarette out of his pack of Lucky Strikes, stuck it in a corner of his mouth and lit it with a Navy Zippo.

Henry came back into the lounge. 'It's for you,' he said to me.

I went out into the passageway and picked up the receiver. It was Alice.

'It's time,' she said. 'Are you packed?'

'So soon? I thought it would be a couple more days.'

'You'll be picked up at five thirty tomorrow morning and taken to the ship,' Alice said.

'OK.'

'Are you packed and ready?'

'Yes, ma'am.'

'Bon voyage, then. Take care.'

'I will.'

She hung up, and I stood in the hall for a few seconds, still holding the telephone receiver.

This was it. It was really happening. I was crossing the Atlantic Ocean in a flimsy cargo ship in the dead of winter during wartime to take up a job in London, a city almost destroyed by German bombings, where shortages of almost everything

16

made living there a constant challenge. I walked back into the silent lounge and met my friends' eyes.

'So,' Phoebe said, 'did you get your orders?'

It would be stupid to dissemble at this point. 'Yes,' I said. 'Tomorrow.' I didn't tell them how early. I hoped to slip away without having to make any more goodbyes. 'Milt, Henry, could you take my footlocker downstairs tonight?'

'Of course,' Henry said. He examined the height of the champagne left in the bottle. 'I think there's enough for us all to have one more swallow,' he said.

Two

I tiptoed down the dark hallway carrying my suitcase and musette bag. I didn't want to wake anyone. All the goodbyes of last night had worn out my nerves. I stopped to leave a letter to Phoebe and Ada on the hall table. There was a paper bag waiting there with my name on it. I guessed what was in it – leftover fried chicken and apple pie, wrapped up tightly in wax paper. Bless her heart; Dellaphine was taking no chance that I'd starve today. Unbuckling my musette bag, I tucked the food inside.

I stood on the sidewalk outside, waiting for my ride. Even with my scarf wrapped around my head and face, and my hat pulled down over my ears, my face was cold. Jiggling on the spot, I glanced up and down the dark empty street. The streetlights were shaded, casting a minimum of light – enough to keep you from tripping over a broken piece of sidewalk, maybe. I'd read there were no streetlights allowed now in London. You had to carry a flashlight everywhere.

It was five twenty-five a.m. when I saw the nondescript black Chevy sedan come around the corner and pull up in front of me. A large colored man in work clothes got out of the driver's seat.

'Lester!' I said.

He grinned at me, showing several gold teeth.

Lester was a messenger and driver at OSS; he knew every shortcut in the city. Our office, the Morale Operations Unit, was just one of many that depended on him.

'Yes, ma'am,' he said. 'At your service.'

I reached out and clasped his hand warmly. 'I'm glad to see you,' I said. 'I didn't get to say goodbye to you on Friday.'

'I'm glad too, Mrs Pearlie. But then Miss Osborne said she didn't trust anyone else to get you to your ship.' He glanced down at my two cases. 'That can't be all you are taking,' he said.

'No, I've got a footlocker inside in the passageway.'

'I'll get it.'

'Be as quiet as you can. I don't want to wake anyone up. I've had all the goodbyes I can handle already.'

I watched Lester stride toward the front door and let himself in quietly. In the next minute I tried to memorize the look of the house where I'd lived for two years. Where my new life as an independent working woman had started. The front stoop, where there was just enough over-hang to shade you from a downpour. The double window in the lounge where Phoebe had hung her Blue Star Mothers banner with two blue stars embroidered on it. The lounge itself – the only room in the house apart from the dining room where we had space enough to gather. Ada and I had surprised Phoebe by making slip-covers for the faded suite of furniture last summer. I had met Joe there the first night I arrived in Washington.

Lester came out of the house, carrying my

19

footlocker easily on one shoulder. He stashed it in the Chevy with my suitcase before opening the car door for me. I scooched into the passenger seat, relieved to get out of the cold. Lester slid into the driver's side.

'So, where are we headed?' I asked.

'Ma'am, you got to tell me,' Lester said, drawing a sealed envelope out of his jacket pocket and handing it to me.

It was a plain envelope with my name scrawled on it in Miss Osborne's harried handwriting. My orders. Opening it, I read the short paragraph. I was to go to the Washington Navy Shipyard and board the SS *Amelia Earhart* bound for Great Britain. In approximately four weeks the ship would dock in Liverpool and someone from OSS would meet me and escort me to London. That was all.

'Well,' I said, 'we need to go to the DC Navy Shipyard.'

'Doggone,' Lester said. 'I was hoping it was Baltimore. I know a place there that makes the best mussel chowder.'

He started the engine and shifted the gears. We pulled away from the curb. I noticed a light on in the kitchen, where Dellaphine would be starting breakfast. It was Monday, so it would likely be Cream of Wheat with canned fruit and toast.

'I've never heard of a ship named after a woman before,' Lester said, as we drove south on Pennsylvania Avenue.

'Well, when you build thousands of Liberty ships and you can only name them after dead people, you've got to dig deep for names,' I said.

I was pleased actually to be assigned to a ship named after Amelia Earhart. She was one of my heroes. 'Did you know there are twenty-some of these ships named after colored people?'

'I did,' Lester said. 'I seen the SS *Booker T. Washington* steaming down the river once. They must have run out of women's names,' he said, chuckling. 'But you know about those Liberty ships, don't you? They're welded instead of riveted.'

Here it came.

'I heard one of them seams didn't hold and a ship just split down the middle and the two halves just sunk,' Lester said, and then chuckled some more.

Liberty ships were built in modules from a British master plan and then welded together. The modules could be adapted to carry passengers, dry cargo or oil and gasoline. The ships were built so quickly and cheaply that no one expected them to last more than a few years.

'You're not scaring me,' I said. 'I'm sure the ship is perfectly safe.' At least, more of them arrived at their destinations than didn't.

As we drove down Pennsylvania Avenue, DC's famous monuments and buildings loomed in the darkness. We passed the State Department and then the White House. It was lit by special lighting designed by General Electric, designed not to cast glare into the house and disturb the residents sleeping, or trying to sleep, in their bedrooms. The watch was changing; two Army trucks were discharging soldiers to take the place of those who'd guarded the President all night.

21

Pennsylvania Avenue swerved south for a bit, passing the massive Treasury Building fronted with tall marble Ionic columns, then angled southeast again. Past the Capital and the Library of Congress. Lester changed gears.

'I'm about to turn on to New Jersey Avenue, Mrs Pearlie,' Lester said. 'Mrs Osborne asked me to make sure you didn't want to change your mind.'

'No, not at all,' I answered. Although my heart rate picked up and my stomach roiled, I was still eager to take up my new assignment.

My first job had been at the Wilmington Shipbuilding Company and I thought I knew what a naval yard would look like, but I wasn't prepared for what I saw when Lester pulled away from the army checkpoint at a government entrance and drove into the Washington Navy Yard. We arrived in time to hear whistles signal the change of shift across the 155-acre yard. Thousands of workers left their posts in more than a hundred buildings and dozens of ships, and thousands more took their place. The streets were packed with men and women, white and black, wearing work clothes and carrying lunch buckets, crowding on to buses to transport them home. Lester and I were stuck in traffic and I just gawked. As dawn broke, the yard's flood-lights cut off.

'I know a shortcut,' Lester said, shifting the car into reverse. He maneuvered away from the parade of buses and turned down a street that paralleled the yard's perimeter fencing.

A few blocks south, the street dead-ended at the Anacostia River. We turned left and drove along its banks until we came to the docks and quays. They seemed to go on forever. Ships of all kinds lined up like sardines in a can, most being loaded with cargo and a few in dry dock being painted or repaired.

Lester stopped next to a colored longshoreman loading a reel of steel cable as thick as his arm on to a cart. A mule with one ear cocked our way was harnessed to the cart, ready to tote the wooden reel on to the nearby dock. He snorted at us, his breath steaming from the cold.

'Do you know where I can find the *Amelia Earhart*?' Lester asked him. 'It's a Liberty ship, supposed to depart today?'

The man pointed further along the waterfront. 'About a mile down,' he said. 'It's almost finished loading.'

The *Amelia Earhart* rocked gently at her berth. I had done a little reading up on Liberty ships once I knew I'd be traveling on one. Sure enough, this one was just as ugly as promised. It had an ungainly hull which accommodated five cargo holds. Three booms and a couple of davits with their dangling winches and chains looked like tall spiders crouching on deck, which was packed tight with jeeps, trucks and even a locomotive. What little room was left on deck was taken by the minimal superstructure amidships which wrapped around the engine stack and held the wheelhouse, the bridge and, below deck, the galley, mess, ward-room and berths for passengers and officers. Like

23

most Liberty ships, this one carried artillery for its defense, a three-inch/fifty millimeter gun at the bow, a five-inch/thirty-millimeter caliber at the stern and eight twenty-millimeter guns that resembled oversized machine guns – two forward, two aft and four amidships. The guns were manned by an Armed Guard – forty or so Navy gunners commanded by an ensign. The crew, commanded by a master, numbered around sixty. The crew were merchant mariners, not members of the military, but with the war some were trained by the Navy.

The water almost reached the Plimsoll line on the *Amelia Earhart*, so it was nearly loaded. One winch maneuvered a crate on to the deck, where a couple of seamen manhandled it into an open hatch to lower it into the hold. Another winch lowered a dangling ambulance on to the deck, where it would be secured with steel cables to steel cleats to prevent it from rolling off the ship and into the sea.

Lester parked the car across the road from the ship in front of a plain brick building, which had the words 'Waiting Rooms' stenciled across the door. 'You can't board until the ship is loaded,' he said. 'Let's see if we can find a warm spot for you to wait.'

We carried my luggage to the waiting room door, which had a sheet of paper stapled to it beneath the sign that read 'Today's Departures' with 'SS *Amelia Earhart*' typed below. Lester opened the door and we went into a large room with benches on two sides with the usual sign over each: 'White' and 'Colored'. A pot-bellied coal stove blazed in a corner. Only one woman waited there, a plain cardboard suitcase by her side, on the 'White' side. She was less than thirty, I thought, dressed in a tweed suit, wool tights and heavy brogues. Her thick wool coat and beret were draped over her suitcase. She was reading a book and didn't even glance at me as I walked over to her.

'Excuse me,' I said, sitting down next to her. 'Are you waiting to board the *Amelia Earhart*?'

'I am,' she said, finally making eye contact. She spoke in a lovely British accent. 'It's still loading cargo. The second mate came by and said it would be several hours before passengers could board.'

'Lester,' I said, as he set down my trunk on the floor next to my other suitcase, 'you go on; I'm fine here.'

'Are you sure?' he said, looking around the room. 'Aren't there any other passengers?'

'There are,' the woman said, 'but they went to the canteen for hot drinks.' She dropped her eyes to a book in her lap, obviously avoiding more conversation.

'I'll go on, then,' Lester said. I reached out and squeezed his hand. 'You take care, hear?' he said.

'You too,' I said. He touched his hat and left the room, letting in a cold blast of air when he opened the door. I stood at a window and watched him hurry to the car through the cold. He was the last person I would see from my former life in DC for a very long time.

The room was completely quiet except for the roar of the fire in the stove. A few minutes passed,

25

and then my companion set her shoulders and looked up as if she had made a decision. She reached out to shake my hand, and I took hers. She had a strong grip.

'My name is Blanche Bryant,' she said.

'I'm Louise Pearlie,' I answered. 'You're English, obviously.'

'Yes, on my way home. I'm from Winchester.'

'I'm from North Carolina, but I've been working for the government in DC for a couple of years.' Neither one of us volunteered any more information. This was wartime, when strangers didn't talk about their jobs or much else, for that matter. We had secrets to keep.

A blast of cold air struck us as a young colored woman, barely more than a girl, came through the door carrying her suitcase and a large purse thrown over her shoulder. She was quite pretty, reminding me of Hazel Scott, the jazz singer. She had those faux bangs you make by rolling up the front of your hair into a fat curl. Another roll rested on her neck, all of it tucked into a knitted Dutch bonnet that covered her neck and ears. Just thinking about how warm it must be made my ears feel even more chilled. She wore a scarf that matched the bonnet's blue-and-gray pattern, a heavy wool coat and thick tights with saddle shoes. She gave Blanche and me a warm smile as she carried her suitcase over to sit on the 'Colored' bench. I smiled back at her and Blanche roused herself enough to nod. But the young woman didn't sit down after she put down her suitcase.

'Ma'am,' she said, coming over to me.

'Yes,' I answered.

26

'Are you traveling on the *Amelia Earhart*?'

'I am. My name is Louise Pearlie.'

'I'm your stewardess, Grace Bell,' she answered. 'That trunk of yours – it needs to go in the ship's hold. There's a cart out front for the hold luggage. Didn't you see it?'

'No,' I answered, and bent over to grab the trunk's handle.

'Let me help you,' she said, taking the other handle. The two of us easily carried the footlocker out into the frigid air where I saw a hand cart clearly labeled for hold luggage for the *Amelia Earhart*. Together, we hoisted my trunk on top of the stack of large trunks and boxes already there.

'Thanks,' I said. 'I don't know how I missed this. I guess I had my head down to avoid the cold. Where are you from?' I'd recognized from Grace's accent that she was from my part of the world.

'Hampstead, North Carolina.'

Just a few miles up the coast from my home. 'I'm from Wilmington. I'm a government girl, been working in DC for a couple of years.'

'I came north after I graduated high school so I could get a decent job. My mother picks crabs for the Hampstead Seafood Company and I didn't want to spend my life doing that.'

Grace held the door open for me and we headed straight for the pot-bellied stove to warm ourselves back up.

'I joined the merchant marine after Pearl Harbor,' Grace said. 'I live with my auntie on U Street. She has a flower shop.'

27

'I didn't know . . .' I said, hesitating.

'That colored women could join the merchant marine? You should know there aren't enough white men to go around these days,' she said, her hazel eyes twinkling. 'When there are women passengers on a merchant ship, you got to have a stewardess to wait on them. Can't have a man draw your bath.'

'Do you know who the passengers are?'

'A Dutch family, husband and wife and two daughters. Then there's a salesman from the American Rubber Company. He's back and forth to England. I've sailed with him before. And an elderly Irishman going home to retire.'

'In the middle of a war?'

'Yeah, I know. It's wacky.' Grace nodded toward Blanche, who'd hadn't moved since we took my trunk outside, except for turning the pages of her book. 'You've met Mrs Bryant.' Grace's tone was a little odd when she mentioned Blanche, enough so that I looked at her quizzically. 'I've traveled with her too, on her voyage here to the States,' Grace said, again in that strange tone of voice that sounded . . . well, not fearful exactly, but wary.

'What about her?' I said, lowering my voice.

Grace shook her head. 'I've said too much already,' she said, moving over to sit down on the 'Colored' bench.

I returned to my own seat. Blanche was so absorbed in her book that I didn't speak to her. I pulled one of the new books I'd purchased out of my musette bag – a P.G. Wodehouse. I'd not read him before. A friend told me his books were

28

quite humorous, and I reckoned I'd need a few smiles as I crossed the Atlantic to take my mind off submarines and storms.

Our little group of what the ship's manifest called 'casual passengers' clustered at the foot of the accommodation ladder, the portable steps winched down from the deck of the ship to the quay, waiting to be permitted on board. I had no difficulty putting faces to the descriptions Grace had given me. The Dutch family were gathered in a small clutch, murmuring to each other. They didn't look a thing like the plump, smiling Dutch boy on the paint can, though. All four of them, both parents and two daughters, were thin and pale. The wife leaned up against her husband as though she was too tired to stand. As if she'd been ridden hard and put up wet, as Merle would have said. The Irishman had to be the compact man with thick shoulders, calloused hands and white hair streaked with faded red. Another woman, whom Grace hadn't mentioned, also waited to board. She wore a WAC winter uniform and a heavy army parka. I knew she was a nurse because of the emblem on her hat and the medical utility bag, marked with a red cross, thrown over her shoulder. I estimated that she was a few years older than me, which would place her in her mid-thirties. There was Blanche, of course. And finally a young man with slicked down hair wearing a heavy coat, fedora and a professional salesman's smile. He was the first to introduce himself.

'I'm Gilbert Fox,' he said, offering his hand to everyone in turn. 'Call me Gil. I work for the

American Rubber Company. This is my third trip across the pond.'

The Irishman touched his worn tweed flat cap. 'Ronan Murphy here. I'm retired. On my way home to Northern Ireland to live with my sister.'

The Dutchman half smiled at the group, his hands gripping his suitcase as if he didn't dare let it go to shake hands. 'Bram Smit,' he said. 'And my wife, Irene, our daughters, Alida and Corrie.' I guessed that Alida was nearly eighteen and Corrie about twelve. 'I hope we are permitted to board soon,' he said, in excellent English. 'We have just gotten off the train from Chicago and we are all very tired.' Indeed, Irene looked as if she was done in. She leaned on her husband's arm, closing her eyes occasionally.

The WAC nurse shook everyone's hand firmly. 'I'm Olive Nunn,' she said. 'I'm on my way to take up a hospital job in England. Don't know what hospital yet, or even where it is. I'm traveling with you because the troop ship I was supposed to take couldn't wait to depart until I got over a case of the flu.'

It was my turn. 'My name is Louise Pearlie,' I said. 'I'm a government file clerk and typist. Going to England to file and type there.'

A sudden gust of wind carrying freezing rain drops blew over, as if to remind us that we were sailing at a very questionable time of year. Our group felt silent, all of us lost in our own thoughts. After a few minutes a grizzled seaman wearing a sou'wester opened the gate to the staircase. 'Time to board,' he said. 'Come on up. The chief steward will meet you in your quarters.'

A couple of crewmen had followed the first to collect our suitcases and tote them up the staircase, leaving us with just our personal bags to carry. It was a good thing, since I doubted most of us could carry a suitcase up the metal stairs. It was too steep and the ship rocked in its berth. Then there was the wind.

As I climbed, I noticed a young man at the foot of the stairs talking to the steward who'd directed us to board. The youth was dressed like a seaman but wasn't from the crew, although he looked as if he wanted the job. He carried a duffle bag over his shoulders. The merchant marine was chronically in need of manpower and our ship was likely short a couple of hands. The young man, his carrot-colored hair sticking out from under his cap, showed some sort of paper to the grizzled seaman, who then gestured him to board the ship. The young man was obviously elated: he jumped up several steps as he mounted the stairs. I guessed he'd been hired.

We scaled the portable staircase, hanging on to the rail for dear life to keep from being blown off. The climb up the side of the ship had to be three stories. By the time we reached the deck, Irene looked as though she couldn't move another step. 'Take your mother's hat box,' Smit said to his older daughter, who rolled her eyes at the request but took her mother's box without verbal complaint.

Following the seamen carrying our suitcases, we threaded our way between the vehicles that crowded the decks. Sometimes the space between them was so narrow we had to turn sideways

31

to get through. At last we reached some open deck space at the first floor of the superstructure, the small part of the ship devoted to people instead of cargo. I knew from my reading about Liberty ships that it contained the wheelhouse, bridge and the captain's cabin. Below deck would be the galley, mess hall and officers' wardroom, berths for the officers, and whatever berths were available for casual passengers – the motley assortment of civilians hitching a ride. Deep below the superstructure was an enormous three-cylinder engine and boiler; its exhaust stack rose right through the superstructure and towered over it.

Liberty ships could be configured in many ways, so there was no telling what we would find when we went below. A seaman opened a metal door and gestured us through. 'The chief steward is waiting for you below,' he said. We went down a metal staircase with a polished wooden handrail into a short passageway that was as cold as the air on deck. I was surprised by the space. Instead of the gray metal I'd expected, the walls and doors gleamed with warm oak. Brass lighting fixtures cast a welcoming glow. The brass handles on the doors and a brass finial on the end of the stair rail looked as if they'd just been polished.

Sure enough, the chief steward, a stocky, bald man, greeted us with the traditional 'Welcome aboard!' We gathered around him, packed in tight in the small space. 'I'm the chief steward of this vessel,' he said. 'My name is Ray Pearce, but you should address me as Chief Pearce or just

Chief. Let me go over a few things before I show you to your berths.'

You could sense us all slump. We were exhausted and wanted to get to our bunks.

'I meant it when I welcomed you to this vessel,' Chief Pearce said, 'but we are at war and you are civilians who know nothing about the operation of this ship. Our job is to get our cargo to Liverpool, not to watch over you. You're not allowed in certain areas of this ship, with no exception. We have five holds loaded with seven thousand eight hundred tons of "C" rations, "D" rations, boxes of thirty-caliber ammunition, crates of seventy-five-millimeter gun shells and hundred-and-five-millimeter Howitzer shells. You have no business being down there. The 'tween deck, which is the space between the ceilings of the holds and the main deck, is also off limits.'

I could hear my fellow passengers gasp. With all those munitions in the holds, if we took a torpedo hit, we wouldn't have much chance of survival, that's for sure. Pearce didn't acknowledge our reaction.

'The *Amelia Earhart* is powered by a hundred-and-forty-ton vertical triple expansion steam engine,' he continued. 'It has countless moving metal parts. The boiler is incredibly hot. Stay out of the engine room. It's dangerous.

'During the day you may gather in the wardroom when it's not being used for meals. You are welcome to walk and smoke on the main deck. Be careful, though. The deck is packed with vehicles. There are cables, chocks, blocks and cleats just waiting to trip you up. And stay

33

away from the gun emplacements. Don't fall overboard because we won't stop even for a minute to search for you. Oh' – and here he gestured toward the staircase – 'this is the only graduated staircase in the place. It was built a while back for a very important passenger who couldn't manage ladders. Otherwise, you'll need to use ladders to get from level to level. Use both hands and be careful. When you're walking down the ship's passageways, keep a hand on a bulwark at all times to help keep your balance. A bulwark is a wall to you.'

Chief Pearce paused for a breath before he continued. 'Your room steward is Grace Bell. She'll look after your berths and run baths and other such personal things for the ladies. Men, you are on your own for your personal needs. There's a lavatory at one end of the hall and a bathroom at the other. You'll be assigned a bath time by Steward Bell. In your room you'll find a life preserver and a bucket. The bucket is for your use until you get your sea legs.'

The chief jangled a handful of keys. 'I'm going to show you to your berths,' he said. 'You'll want to unpack and rest, I'm sure. Dinner is at six o'clock. You'll need to go down the ladder at the end of this passageway; there's a passageway parallel to this one, and the mess is through the door at the end of the hall. You'll see seamen going in. Go through the mess line with them, but civilian passengers eat in the officers' ward-room. You can sit anywhere except the master's table. You'll see where to go.' The chief picked a set of keys out of his handful. 'Mr and Mrs

Smit, this room here connects to the one next door. These are yours and your daughters' rooms.' Smit took the keys as if they were the Holy Grail. He unlocked the door and he and his family almost fell inside.

The chief didn't waste time allocating our rooms and giving out the rest of our keys. I found myself fitting my key into an oak door between the two other women, Blanche and Olive. The two men, Gil and Ronan, were across the hall from us, next to the Smits.

I actually didn't need my key, because inside my berth I found Grace Bell tucking in the sheets of my bunk. She was singing 'Sweet Georgia Brown' softly to herself.

'You have a lovely voice,' I said to her.

She turned around. 'Thank you, ma'am,' she said. 'I do love to sing.'

Grace had changed into a heavy wool dress, knit coat, wool stockings and her saddle shoes, but she was just as pretty as when I met her in the waiting room. Even dressed as she was, she had a slim figure, a lovely smile, a fashionable hairdo and nice makeup. Most men would call her a knockout.

My berth was tiny. Between the two of us and my suitcase, we could barely move.

'Welcome, Mrs Pearlie,' she said. 'Let me put your towels under your sink and I'll be done and leave you to rest. Let me show you where your life jacket and bucket are. And just so you're prepared, there will be a lifeboat drill sooner rather than later.'

She opened a door to a small cabinet fastened

35

to the bulwark near the head of my bunk. 'Here they are,' she said, gesturing to the bucket and life preserver. 'Do you get seasick, ma'am?'

'Sometimes,' I said. These seas were going to be rougher than any I'd experienced in a fishing boat off the coast of North Carolina.

'I've got some ginger if you need it,' she said.

The top of the cabinet served as a nightstand. A small reading lamp and a metal ashtray were screwed to it. I didn't smoke, but the ashtray would be a good place to leave my glasses, watch and Phoebe's ring at night.

'Did the chief steward tell you when dinner would be ready?' Grace asked. 'Lunch is long over, I'm afraid.'

I remembered the bag of leftovers Dellaphine had put on the hall table for me and felt my empty stomach urge me to eat. 'I've got my lunch with me,' I said.

Grace tucked towels and a washcloth in a cabinet which held the tiniest sink I'd ever seen. It wasn't much bigger than a cereal bowl. 'Hot water?' I asked.

Grace straightened up. 'Sorry,' she said, 'just cold. But you will be able to take a hot bath every day, thanks to the engine boiler. The women are supposed to take their baths in the morning, the men at night. I'd suggest seven fifteen. That way you can sleep until seven, and since breakfast is at eight, you can get dressed and get your coffee right away.'

'That sounds good,' I said.

'You can wash your undies and stockings in the bath with you, too.'

36

I hadn't taken my coat and hat off yet. 'When will they turn on the heat?' I asked.

'Oh,' Grace said, 'I'm so sorry. There's no heat.'

I must have misunderstood her. 'What did you say?' I asked.

'The only spaces in the ship that are heated are the mess hall and wardroom.'

'You're joking,' I said.

'I wish I was,' she said. 'But this ship was fitted for a southern run and hasn't been upgraded. And it won't be. We must ration fuel. You'll just have to wear layers of clothes. You have plenty of blankets and the exhaust stack from the engine goes right through the center of the superstructure. So once we're underway it's not quite as cold as it is outside.'

No wonder Grace was bundled up. 'I'm going to need to get my trunk out of the hold. My heaviest clothes are inside,' I said.

Grace hid a smile behind a hand. 'You can't reach your trunk, Mrs Pearlie. It's locked in a cage in the hold surrounded by boxes of ammunition. But when the bosun's store opens in the morning, you might be able to pick up some warm clothes. They'll be seamen's work clothes, though.'

I was exhausted. I'd gotten out of my cozy bed at four thirty in the morning, driven across DC to the Navy Yard, sat on hard benches in a waiting room for hours, finally got to my cabin, only to find I'd be crossing the icy Atlantic Ocean without heat. I was hungry and sleepy.

'When you're done unpacking, leave your suitcase in the hall and I'll store it for you,' Grace

37

said. There was certainly nowhere to put it in my tiny cabin.

'Oh,' she said, turning as she was halfway out of my room, 'I bring coffee, tea and cookies down every day at four o'clock. We have a great ship's baker.'

After Grace left, I felt all my pent-up excitement and anticipation drain away. I quickly unpacked the contents of my suitcase into the drawer set in the base of my bunk. I was angry that no one told me I would need my arctic parka and wool gloves on board ship. I hated to think I'd need to sleep in my good wool coat. It had a real fur collar and it took me months to pay off my Woodies' charge account after I'd bought it. If I wore it constantly for weeks at sea, it would be ruined by salt spray. Not to mention that it wasn't going to be warm enough.

My musette bag with my personal items fit neatly into the drawer with my clothing and my tin of pralines. I put my big suitcase out in the hall. I didn't hear a sound from my neighbors. Everyone must have been napping. Back in my room, I crawled into my bunk in my coat and wrapped two blankets around myself. Opening the brown paper bag Dellaphine had sent with me, I found fried chicken, a biscuit and apple pie. And a napkin. A cloth napkin, one of Phoebe's many in a rose pattern. Phoebe loved roses. I would keep the napkin. It brought back good memories.

The first piece of cold fried chicken I unwrapped was gone in about three bites. The second piece I savored, knowing how long it might be before I ate fried chicken again. Dellaphine had packed two pieces of apple pie. I ate one and tucked the other one, rewrapping it in wax paper, into the small drawer of what passed as a bedside table. While eating, I had warmed up considerably, and when I lay down, I fell sound asleep.

I awoke to the sound of conversation and the rattle of dishes in the passageway. The coffee and tea must have arrived. Throwing my blankets off, I freshened up at the tiny sink in my cabin and went out into the hall. I found a clutch of my shipmates gathered around a pull-down table with tea, coffee and cookies in the passageway near the foot of the ladder. The table was hinged on one side so it could be stored flat against the bulwark, since you couldn't possibly carry a table down the stairs.

Mr Smit was balancing four cups of tea and a stack of cookies on a makeshift tray, the lid of his wife's hatbox, to take back to his family. Ronan Murphy had drained his first cup of tea already and stood expectantly, waiting for us.

'Ladies,' Ronan said, 'will you be drinking tea or coffee?'

'Coffee,' Olive and I answered in unison.

'Aha! Lucky for me,' he said. 'I can have another cuppa.' He emptied the teapot into his cup.

'Anyone up for a game of cards?' Gil asked.

'Not now,' I said. 'Maybe some other time.'

'I'm still knackered,' Ronan said. 'I'm going to rest in my cabin and read a copy of the *Irish Times* I found at a newsstand at the train station. I'll see you all at dinner.' He carefully balanced his full cup as he went back to his berth.

'Is your wife feeling better?' I asked Smit.

'Much,' he said. 'She's napped all afternoon. So have the girls.' He turned and walked gingerly down the hall toward his cabin, taking care not to tip his tray.

Gil and Olive stood at the table lacing their coffee with cream and sugar and adding cookies to their saucers. Gil still wore his heavy topcoat with a long scarf wrapped around his neck and over his head. Thick wool gloves stuck out of his pocket. Olive had on her army arctic parka. It was identical to the one packed in my trunk, unreachable in the hold.

'How did you two know the ship isn't heated?' I asked.

'I've crossed before on business,' Gil said. 'On this very ship, in fact.'

'And I got a list from WAC HQ on what I would need on the crossing,' Olive said. I'd had a list too, but it didn't warn me about lack of heat. Was I just supposed to have guessed that the ship wouldn't be heated? When I wrote my first letter to Alice Osborne, she was going to hear about this.

'The coffee is still hot,' Olive said, holding up the coffee pot. 'It will warm you up. You know, you might be able to find something warmer than the coat you're wearing in the bosun's stores. And wool socks and mittens.'

'I hope so,' I said, filling my cup with steaming coffee. 'Would you like to join me in my berth for a chat?' I asked.

'Love to,' she said.

* * *

40

We wrapped up in my blankets on my bunk and sipped on our coffee, which was quite good. No added chicory, thank goodness. Olive dipped her oatmeal cookies in her coffee, but I liked to crunch mine. She glanced at my left hand. 'I see that you are single, too. Are you an old maid like me?' she asked lightheartedly.

'I'm a widow,' I said. 'For several years now. My husband died before the war.'

'I'm so sorry! He must have been very young.'

'He was. He contracted pneumonia after a case of the measles.' My husband was a Western Union telegrapher and was exposed to dozens of people every day. A customer brought her sick children into the office to send a telegraph to her mother, asking her to come help her, and that was all it took for my husband to catch his death.

'Is that your engagement ring?' she asked, gesturing toward Phoebe's ring on my right hand. 'It's lovely.'

'No, it's a gift from my landlady,' I said. 'So why are you not hitched?'

Olive had finished her coffee and put the cup down so she could draw her gloves back on. 'Dearie,' she said. 'I had an engagement go very wrong. Horribly wrong. Gothic novel wrong.'

'I'm sorry!'

'He married my sister instead. Really, I thought I would die. Instead, I left home and enrolled in nursing school so I could support myself. It was the best thing that ever happened to me. I love nursing. I don't mind being unmarried at all anymore. Do you have a beau?'

41

'I do. I did. But then he was transferred and I don't know where. He's not allowed to write.'

'How awful! And I can tell by the look on your face that you care deeply for him.'

'Yes,' I said, 'I do. But I decided not to mope, so I took this assignment.' I focused on flicking crumbs off myself and then took both our empty cups out to the gangway to put on the table for Grace to pick up. I didn't want Olive to see my eyes.

We agreed to meet at the foot of our staircase to go to dinner.

'How many bells ring for dinner?' I asked. The ship's bells rang constantly, with no rhyme or reason that I could tell.

'I have no idea. I just look at my watch. Six o'clock.'

'Should I knock on Blanche's door and invite her to join us?'

'I wouldn't. She's awfully unfriendly. Almost rude. She's made it clear she wants to be left alone, so let's honor her wishes.'

'You're right; she doesn't want our company.' I wondered what had happened to make Blanche so hard.

I laid out all my clothing on my bed, figuring out what combination of items would keep me the warmest. Darn it! I had packed for a heated living area and I felt like a fool. How was I to have known? In the end I kept on my cotton knit stockings, pulled on long underwear, a blouse – what a useless item to bring – and buttoned my favorite hand-knit cardigan over it. That

42

cardigan was a shade of blueberry that reminded me of the only evening dress I had ever owned. Finally, I pulled on socks over my stockings and shoved my feet into saddle shoes. I could just imagine how disgusting all this would be if I wore it for days! But then I guessed I wouldn't be alone. And Grace had said I could wash my underclothes when I took my bath.

I met Olive at the foot of the staircase. Together we found the ladder at the end of the passageway, descended safely and followed the scent of food until we found ourselves in line at the mess hall. The seamen wore no discernible uniforms, just heavy winter work clothes. But all of them had thick knitted watch caps and wool mittens shoved into their pants pockets. The Navy Armed Guard were easy to spot. They wore actual uniforms and carried sidearms. They were the only people on board who were allowed to carry guns and man the artillery on deck.

As we passed down the line, messmen wearing aprons over their jackets slapped food on metal trays for us exactly as they did for the seaman. Since we'd just left port, it looked as if some of the food was fresh – beef tips on real mashed potatoes, but canned corn and peas, and real milk. Rolls and butter, of course. I passed on dessert – chocolate pudding – since I had Dellaphine's pie and pralines back in my cabin. We tried to speak to the seamen in line, but they were decidedly frosty toward us.

Olive and I went down the narrow space between the mess tables, which were already lined with seamen as tightly as sardines in a can, until we saw the door labeled 'Wardroom', which served as the officers' mess during meals. We pushed it open and found a small crowded space with six tables and their chairs screwed to the floor. There was some sign of rank in here, mostly emblems on jacket sleeves and watch caps. The master, or captain, sat at the table near a double porthole with men I assumed were his officers. Gil was there, too. He must have had an invitation. Olive and I moved toward a far table where the Smits and Blanche were seated, but we were waylaid by the ensign in command of the Navy Armed Guard. I knew he was an ensign because of the single star on his uniform lapel and the gunnery emblem on his shirt.

'Ladies,' he said, 'please sit with us. We would be honored.' There were two other men at his table wearing naval winter deck gear, with their heavy coats hung over the backs of their chairs. I recognized the emblems on their coats: one was a radio operator and one a signalman. They stood up for us; the ensign pulled out my chair and the signalman seated Olive. I felt a little embarrassed, but the ensign was quite handsome and polite, even if he was a bit forward.

Once seated, the ensign introduced himself. 'Ensign Thomas Bates, ma'am, at your service. Everyone calls me Tom. This is Signalman Fred Wilson, one of our radiomen. Our unit has three radiomen, and they are all answerable to "Sparky".' The men looked very young, even the ensign. Almost ten years younger than me, I guessed.

One good thing about eating with the military,

I could see their surnames on their pockets. The merchant mariners wore patches on their work jackets that told me if they were assigned to the deck, engine or the steward, but that was all.

When we sat down, the three men passed us salt and pepper and butter and filled our water glasses. Olive and I accepted their manners with grace, and soon we were talking as we ate. 'So where are you from?' Tom asked us. Olive and I answered their questions while revealing as little personal information as we could. There were few women on board and we didn't want to be the subject of conversation among the men.

'And you?' I asked, after Olive and I had finished our short biographies.

'I'm from Newport News,' Tom said. 'This is a new assignment for me. I don't know these men myself yet. They've just finished training.'

'I'm from Brooklyn, ma'am,' Sparky said. 'And Signalman Oates here is from Chicago.'

'You've come a long way, then,' I said to Oates.

'Not as far as some – my brother's in the Pacific.'

'Well, I'm glad you're here to protect us,' Olive said.

'We're responsible for guarding the entire ship,' Tom said, 'not just the people on it. Our boys in England desperately need the cargo we're carrying, and the ship needs to stay afloat too, and make as many crossings as possible. I don't mean to demean the value of human life, but the cargo and ship are just as important as the people on board.'

'I saw the guns as we boarded,' I said. 'Somehow it doesn't seem like enough.'

'They have to be,' Tom said. 'There's only so much room on deck. And remember, we'll join a convoy in Halifax. We'll have other cargo ships with us in a protected formation, flanked by warships, with air support. We'll be in a slow convoy – a Liberty ship can only steam at about nine and a half knots. But we'll make it.'

'Did I hear you say Halifax?' I asked. 'Is that Halifax, Nova Scotia?'

'Yeah,' Sparks answered. 'A little over six hundred miles from here.'

Oh my God. We'd be at a latitude of over forty degrees! How much colder would it be there?

'You look a little pale,' the signalman said to me. 'Are you all right?'

'No one told Mrs Pearlie that most of the ship isn't heated,' Olive said. 'How cold is it in Halifax about this time of year?'

'It ranges from fifteen degrees to maybe thirty,' Sparky said. 'Colder on the water, of course.'

'Didn't you bring warm clothes?' Tom asked me.

'Of course I did,' I said. 'They're in my trunk in the hold – unreachable. I didn't think I'd need them until I got to England.' I didn't want my shipmates to think I was chicken, so I quickly added, 'I'm fine. I've got a wool coat back in my berth and I'll just layer up. It's not like I'll have to take a deck watch or anything.'

The bells that signaled the end of the dinner hour sounded. 'Thank you for asking us to sit with you,' Olive said. 'The way the ordinary seamen in line acted, we didn't feel too welcome.

As if they'd prefer not to have passengers on the ship.'

'It's an old sailor's superstition that women on board ship bring bad luck,' Sparky said. 'And, of course, women and children have to be evacuated in the first lifeboat if the ship needs to be abandoned. That means the seamen themselves have to wait to evacuate until after the first lifeboat is successfully launched.'

'And the seamen aren't allowed to curse in your presence,' Tom said, smiling. 'That cuts their vocabulary in half.'

I thought Olive and I handled that little bit of information well, but perhaps our smiles were just a bit forced.

As the wardroom emptied, Tom turned to me. 'Would you like to go up on the bridge deck? You can see the entire ship from there, and there's a waxing moon tonight.'

'Yes, I would. But I need to go back to my cabin and get my coat.'

'I'm sure Signalman Oates will lend you his coat,' he said. 'He's off duty now and I'll get it back to him.'

'Absolutely,' Oates said, holding the coat for me while I slipped it on. I buttoned up the thick waterproof jacket.

'Tell you what, Signalman,' I said, 'I'll give you a hundred dollars for this coat.'

'Sorry, ma'am, there's not enough money for me to give up that coat. Not in this weather.'

I wondered what time the bosun's store opened in the morning.

'The bridge deck is two levels up,' Tom said.

I grabbed at the handrails of both ladders and easily scrambled up them. When we reached the bridge level, Tom knocked on the metal door. A seaman opened the door and we entered.

'Good evening, Deck Cadet,' Tom said to the seaman. Then he turned to the captain. 'Master Jacobs,' he said, 'can I show Mrs Pearlie our route?'

'Certainly,' the master said, 'come in.'

I was surprised by the bridge. You could barely see outside. There was only a tiny square window looking out over the ocean. The wheel occupied most of the floor space. The bulwarks were lined with mysterious instruments with dials the size of dinner plates. The master was bent over a screen glowing green next to the wheel.

The master was much older than I had realized when I noticed him in the wardroom, but he seemed fit and moved well. His face was deeply furrowed by wrinkles, his hands swollen from arthritis. When he took off his cap, he had little hair. His eyebrows made up for it, though – thick, white and wizardish-looking. I guessed that he had come out of retirement when the war started. The captain's cap he wore was the only thing that differentiated him from an ordinary seaman. It was a worn blue peaked captain's hat with the emblem of the merchant marine, an anchor fouled with rope and framed by a wreath. Otherwise, he dressed in the same winter work clothes as his subordinates.

'Welcome, Mrs Pearlie,' the master said. 'This is my first mate, Chief Harley Pitts, at the wheel, and navigating on this watch is Deck Cadet

Willis.' I knew that the first mate was the master's second-in-command and in charge of the deck seamen. He was nearly as old as the master, but a much smaller, almost wizened man. He gripped the wheel with the wiry muscles of a man who'd steered a ship for many years. His forearms bulged like Popeye's and a pipe jutted from the corner of his mouth.

The deck cadet, a young man with a crew cut whose nervous look broadcast that he was in training, moved away from the chart table so that Tom could show it to me. 'Here we are,' he said, pointing to a spot a few miles east of Washington. 'We'll steam along the coast,' he said, tracing our path with his forefinger – north, of course, to Halifax. 'We'll join the other ships meeting there, then cruise to St John's, Newfoundland, where we'll join the main convey. From there we'll set course for England. It will take us about nineteen days if all goes well.'

Popeye snorted. 'That doesn't count the time we'll be docked in Halifax. Three days at least.'

That was good news. I could go ashore and buy warmer clothes!

'Let's go on out to the bridge deck,' Tom said. The bridge deck was an open space where the bridge crew could have a full clear view of the ship's deck and the ocean. Another navigational map was under glass at a small table. A telescope was mounted on the rail.

Outside, despite the wind and cold, the view of the ocean and sky was magnificent. The ocean was ink-colored, crossed with streams of azure. Foam churned by choppy waves sparkled in the moonlight. The waxing moon shone brightly and I could see on every side the silhouettes of other ships cruising north with us, their running lights aglow. Thousands of stars blinked in the sky. When I grasped the railing, it was encased in ice that penetrated my thin kid gloves.

'The other ships near us,' I said. 'Are they headed to Halifax, too?'

'Probably,' he said, 'they're either other cargo ships or warship escorts.' He opened a metal box secured to the rail and pulled out a pair of binoculars, raising them to his eyes. 'Let's see if I can tell.' As he scanned the water Tom's shoulders stiffened. Turning to me, he took my arm. 'I see something I need to report to the captain immediately,' he said, 'we must return to the bridge now.'

Once inside, Tom spoke before the others had time to turn to him. 'Master,' he said, 'I think I saw a submarine.'

'Really?' the master said, turning to him. 'What makes you think that?'

'A silver cigar-shape near the surface. Moving.' My heart rate ticked up, while the deck cadet went rigid. 'Should we sound to quarters, sir?' the cadet asked.

'Let me take a look first,' the master said. 'The sea can look mighty funny in the moonlight.' He reached for another pair of binoculars and followed Tom outside.

Popeye calmly continued to steer the boat. 'What do you think?' the cadet asked him. 'Think there's a submarine out there?'

'One good thing about having an old master,'

Popeye said, 'he's already seen everything twice. Wait and see what he tells us when he gets back.'

I cleaned my glasses before peering out of a narrow window at the two men on the bridge deck, trying to determine from their posture what was happening. Tom was standing almost at attention with his binoculars raised to his eyes, but the master was relaxed, leaning over the rail, staring out over the sea, with just his naked eyes cupped between his hands, his binoculars hanging around his neck. He straightened up and clapped Tom on the back. As they turned to come back inside, I slipped away from the window so they wouldn't notice me there.

The two men reentered the bridge. 'It was a school of fish,' Tom said. 'Right under the surface. As they turned in unison, the moonlight reflected off them so it looked like a large object cruising under the water.'

'Told you,' Popeye said. 'An old man – that's who you want to captain a ship.'

'I'm younger than you, you old sea dog,' the master replied. 'You just stay your course.'

'Yes, sir.'

Back in my room, it felt like midnight instead of nine o'clock at night, or, as I should be thinking now, twenty-one hundred hours. I was knackered, as Ronan would say. It had been one of the longest days of my life, longer even than the day of my young husband's funeral. I'd risen in the dark, driven through Washington, waited on hard benches in a waiting room for hours, climbed a staircase to the *Amelia Earhart* that felt like

51

scaling a mountain, unpacked, met my shipmates, dealt with frigid temperatures and held my breath through a possible submarine sighting.

Sitting on my bunk, I had to talk myself into undressing before falling asleep. I pulled off my wool trousers and exchanged my stockings for long underwear and drew on corduroy dungarees. That was about the extent of my undressing. I'd take my stockings to the bathroom tomorrow and wash them out, and wear my second pair while the first dried. That way maybe I could stay somewhat ahead of my dirty laundry. I cleaned my eyeglasses, crusted with ice and salt spray, at my tiny sink. I'd need to be very careful not to scratch them.

Wanting to conserve my gin, I decided to have a praline instead of a drink. As I bit into it, I sensed the warmth and welcome of Dellaphine's kitchen, but that didn't last long and intense sadness quickly overwhelmed me. Why on earth had I agreed to do this? I did my bit for the war effort in DC. I had friends. I was warmer. Joe could return to DC at any time and I wouldn't be there. Heck, I might not live through the crossing – what was the point of that?

After allowing myself an extensive pity party, I pulled myself together. I had considered all this when I was making my decision to accept the post in England. I was on my way there, and I would make the best of it.

I brushed my teeth and washed my face in my tiny sink, then went down the hall to the head, which, I discovered, had a porthole opened to the outside air for ventilation. The air coming in was arctic and blew directly on my bare backside. Back in my room, I slipped into my bunk and warmed up quickly. I fell asleep anticipating nine hours of sleep before taking a hot bath in the morning.

Three

The ship's horn screeched me wide awake at midnight. Was this the lifeboat drill that Grace had warned me to expect, or was this the real deal? Had the master misinterpreted Tom's sighting after all? As I pulled on my coat and shoes, I didn't hear any artillery fire, so this had to be a drill. Didn't it? I dragged my life jacket out of its cupboard and threw it over my head, fastening the straps, then blundered into the hall where I met my fellow passengers milling about in chaos, shouting and fastening their life jackets while the siren continued to sound.

Gil hopped on to the first step of the staircase. 'Listen to me, I've done this before!' he shouted. He pointed to the Smits. 'Mr Smit, get your wife and daughters up this staircase and climb the next ladder to the boat deck. There'll be a seaman there to show you to your lifeboat.' Smit and his family edged past Gil and hurried up the stairway. 'Next, the women,' Gil said. Olive and I were ready to go, but Blanche wasn't anywhere to be seen. 'Rouse up Mrs Bryant, for God's sake,' Gil said. 'We could be blown out of the water any minute.' Olive and I pounded on her door, screaming her name, but she didn't answer. Her door was unlocked and when I pushed it open, her berth was empty.

I turned to Gil. 'She's not here!'

'Come on, then,' he said. 'Up, up!'

Olive and I surged up the stairway, followed by Gil and Ronan. 'Where do you think Blanche is?' I shouted to Olive, trying to drown out the sound of the siren and running feet overhead. 'Maybe in the wardroom?' she shouted back. 'Maybe smoking on deck? We'll soon find out.'

The seaman waiting for us as we emerged on to the boat deck was not pleased with us. He seemed to have forgotten that he wasn't supposed to curse around women. 'You slackers,' he shouted, 'you're bloody slow! Get to boat number six now; you should have been there five minutes ago!'

The master and Chief Popeye were waiting for us when we joined the Smits at our lifeboat. Grace waited there, too. I guess that the 'women and children first' rule also applied to her. 'If this was a real call to abandon ship, half of us might have drowned by now, thanks to you,' the master said to our woebegone little group. 'Are you aware of the cargo we're carrying? Enough munitions to blow us all to hell and back.'

'I'm sorry, Master, we couldn't find Mrs Bryant,' Gil said.

'Next time, don't wait or look for anyone; just move, if you don't want to drown down below,' the master said.

The youngest Smit daughter, Corrie, started to cry.

The master's fury abated a little. 'Darlin',' he said to her, 'this is for your sake. Wherever you are when you hear that siren, you head for this lifeboat. Don't even wait for your parents or your sister – you hear me? You can meet them here.'

55

She nodded, sniffling back her tears while her mother calmed her, speaking to her softly in Dutch.

'Now,' the master said, turning to Popeye, 'where is Mrs Bryant?'

'Unaccounted for, sir,' he answered.

The master became so red with rage that I worried he might have a heart attack.

'I'm right here, sir,' Blanche said, appearing by my side wearing her life preserver.

'Where the hell have you been?' the master said.

'If you must know, I was in the head,' Blanche answered calmly. 'I got here as fast as I could.'

The master seemed a bit startled by her reference to the toilet. 'You do realize that if you don't make it to this boat in an emergency, we might have to leave you behind?' he said to her. 'If you're not here on time for the next drill, I'll be forced to maroon you in Halifax.'

'Yes, sir, I understand. I'll take my chances just like everyone else. You go on and abandon me if you must. I don't have much to lose.'

Corrie started to sniffle again.

The master didn't answer Blanche directly. Turning to the first mate, he said, 'Stand down.' Popeye shouted the order through a bullhorn and the seamen began to disperse. The terrible noise of the siren stopped.

Grace leaned into our group. '"Stand down" means return to your quarters and sleep in your life preservers,' she whispered. Then she touched Corrie Smit's shoulder. 'Would you like me to bring you and your sister some hot chocolate?'

The girls nodded and their father said, 'Yes, please.'

We trooped down to our quarters, chatting, except for Blanche, who went into her room without a word. A few minutes later, on my way to the lavatory, I saw Grace descending the stairway with a small tray holding two mugs of hot chocolate balanced between her right arm and her waist. With her left hand she grasped the handrail. Our stairway in the passenger area was much less steep than the ladders, and she skittered down it very quickly.

'Be careful,' I said to her. She flashed me a gay smile as she knocked on the Smits' door.

'Yes, ma'am,' she said.

I found that it wasn't difficult at all to fall asleep wearing a life preserver.

Four

I luxuriated in my hot bath the next morning. I had an entire half hour to feel warm before I had to dress. I'd already washed my undies and a pair of stockings, but didn't see how I could wash my sweaters or trousers and get them dry. They'd be ready to walk off the ship on their own when we finally docked in Liverpool. As I drifted off into a daydream, I heard, far away, the thump of artillery. Since there were no sirens, I guessed one of the escort warships must be holding gunnery drills. I suddenly imagined a torpedo or an artillery shell crashing into the ship near the bathroom while I lay in the tub naked. I envisioned a team of rough seamen finding me that way, either dead in the tub or alive treading water. That got me out of the tub! I dressed hurriedly in my only fresh pair of stockings, clean underwear and the same sweater and trousers I had worn the day before. Within minutes I was flying down the passageway to my berth with my hair wrapped in a towel and my wet laundry clutched to me. I never relaxed in the bathtub again.

Olive and I stood together in the breakfast line. The menu chalked on a menu board looked delicious. It turned out that 'fresh eggs to order' didn't exactly mean that. When I requested two scrambled eggs, the colored cook flashed a smile that was missing a couple of teeth. 'That means one egg, over easy or sunny side up,' he said. 'Take your pick.' I chose one egg over easy. The cook broke four eggs at a time, two in each hand, and dropped them on to a grill. The eggs reached from one end of the grill to the other, from raw to done. Another cook flipped them halfway through the process, then slid them on to plates. A messman added bacon and toast. In no time Olive and I had our meals and headed to the officers' mess in the wardroom.

We joined Gil and Ronan at a table. 'Where are the others?' Olive asked.

'I think the Smits are still asleep,' Gil said, 'recovering from seasickness. Blanche is probably adding eye of newt to a cauldron somewhere.'

'That's unkind, mate,' Ronan said.

'It certainly is,' Olive said. 'You don't know what that woman has been through.'

'I do,' Gil said. 'Her husband died on the way over to the States. On this very ship.'

That got my attention. I paused in the midst of enjoying my egg, which was perfectly cooked despite its assembly-line production.

'How do you know that?' I asked.

'I sailed with them. We left Liverpool three months ago. I had to return to the States to be briefed on some new products by my company. Blanche and her husband and his orderly were on board. He was an American and they were returning to his home.'

'He was injured, then?' Olive asked.

'Yeah, he was injured. He was a US Army Air Force pilot. He lost the use of both his legs in a

59

plane crash and wound up in a wheelchair. He wasn't very heroic about it, either. He was angry and nasty to his orderly and his wife. Sometimes you'd see him up on deck, the orderly pushing his wheelchair. They'd sit next to the rail and smoke. But if you tried to engage him in small talk, or ask him to play cards or something, he would refuse. Rather brusquely.'

'Poor man,' I said, thinking of Milt and his struggle to adjust to the loss of his arm.

'Poor Blanche,' Olive said. 'What a bad spot to be in. How did her husband die? Did he have other injuries?'

'He killed himself.'

Just then Blanche entered the officers' mess with her tray. She saw us, but deliberately turned away and found an empty table to occupy. I didn't blame her. I'd been widowed myself, and socializing was the last thing I had wanted to do for months. And my husband hadn't committed suicide.

'How did a bloke who couldn't walk kill himself?' Ronan asked.

'He and the orderly were out on deck. But the orderly went back inside to get a cigarette lighter.'

'Oh, no,' Olive said. 'He shouldn't have left him.'

'Eddie – Eddie Bryant was the pilot's name – rolled himself over to the rail and to the gate where the portable stairway is moored. He unlatched the gate and rolled himself right off the ship. Of course, when the orderly came back, he wasted minutes trying to find him, and once the alarm was raised it was too late to do anything.

60

The master wouldn't have turned back to look for him anyway, but the rest of the convoy was alerted to keep a lookout. Eddie was deep in Davy Jones's locker by then. Still buckled in his wheelchair, I bet.'

'How awful,' I said.

Gil leaned over the table and whispered to us. 'There were some who suggested Blanche pushed Bryant overboard herself. She was out on deck at the time, smoking somewhere. It would have been easy. He was helpless in that chair. She could have pushed him right off the deck. With the wind and waves, no one would have heard him crying for help.'

I glanced over at Blanche. She ate silently, with her eyes fixed on her plate, and red rising up her neck. She must have guessed that we were talking about her. I was angry with Gil for gossiping. I felt sorry for her.

'Stop it, Gil,' I said. 'You don't know that's what happened, do you? Have you got any evidence?'

Gil shrugged. 'There weren't any witnesses,' he said. 'But it could have happened that way. I'm not the only one who thought so.'

'And people think Ireland is full of leprechauns and pots of gold,' Ronan said. 'But we haven't found any yet. Leave the lass alone.'

Reprimanded, Gil fell silent. So did Ronan, Olive and I. We finished our meal and didn't stay at the table for more coffee. I felt slightly dirtied by the conversation and determined to be nice to Blanche even if she was cold to me.

* * *

61

I had misinterpreted the words 'bosun's store'. I thought the boatswain had a shop – you know, where you could buy stuff. It was more like a library. When we ducked into the space over the bow after a cold, windy trek from amidships, we found shelves and hooks filled with everything from coils of rope to mops and wrenches, presided over by a bosun's mate too tall to stand upright in the space. Nothing had a price tag on it and there was no clothing in sight.

'Ladies,' the bosun's mate said, 'do you be looking for something?'

'I'm sorry,' I said, 'I thought this was a store. That sells warm clothes?'

The mate chuckled. 'No, ma'am, this is storage for the equipment the seamen need to do their chores on the ship. They come get what they need and bring it back here. Otherwise, all our tools would go missing. I can see that a landlubber might be confused by the name, though.'

'I grew up on the east coast, so I should have known.'

'What were you ladies looking for? Perhaps I could help.'

'My friend was hoping to find a warm coat and hat,' Olive said.

'I can see that you'd rather not dirty that pretty coat,' the mate said to me, eyeing what I was wearing. It might already be ruined, I thought. I'd picked up an oil smear when the ship had listed and I fell up against a jeep on our trek across the deck. 'What you want is the Lost and Found.'

The mate led us deeper into the crowded space

until we came to a set of shelves stuffed with clothing, including coats. 'We keep whatever we find on the ship after a voyage is over. Sometimes seamen sign on for a trip without the right gear in their duffels. You can pick out whatever works for you and return it before you debark.'

Olive and I pawed through the clothing. The only coat I could find small enough and clean enough for me was a classic navy wool peacoat, the kind sailors had been wearing forever. It was twice as thick as my coat, had a rolled collar I could pull up around my neck, and every one of its big buttons. It fell past my knees. I threw off my coat and pulled on the peacoat. Instantly, I felt warmer. A slight odor of cigarette smoke wafted off it, but I didn't care.

'This seems fairly clean,' Olive said, handing me a seaman's watch cap – a black wool knitted hat I could pull over my ears. Just a few of its previous owner's hairs adhered to the inside. I picked them off and pulled the cap on.

'You look like an able-bodied seaman yourself now,' the bosun's mate said. 'You might find someone ordering you to swab the deck!'

As Olive and I trudged back to our quarters, a group of seamen grinned and touched their caps, hollering out to us. We couldn't understand much of what they said, but apparently they were amused that I was wearing a seaman's clothes. I'd already noticed what a motley assortment of men the ordinary and able-bodied seamen were. They were all colors and several nationalities, as attested by the accents I'd overhead. I recognized a melodic Caribbean voice, and one who shouted out to me had a British accent. Maybe I'd made a couple of friends aboard ship who wouldn't frown at me in the chow line.

We weren't interested in staying outside on the deck for long. A thick, wet fog had fallen overnight and enveloped us. We couldn't see any of the ships sailing nearby, or see their running lights, but we could hear their foghorns signaling their location.

We were about to duck into the door to our quarters when I saw Blanche sitting on a wooden cable spool near the rail, smoking and staring out to sea. She was bundled up in a tweed coat with a scarf tied around her head and had pulled a sou'wester over the scarf to repel the salty spray. She gripped a gold cigarette lighter and a packet of cigarettes in her lap.

'Let's go talk to Blanche,' I said. The well-brought-up Southern girl in me felt the need to make an effort to be kind to this unhappy woman. If she rebuffed me, fine.

'You go ahead,' Olive said. 'Not me. I'm freezing and wet. Let me take your good coat to your cabin and I'll see you later.'

Blanche attempted a smile when she saw me approach and scooted aside so I could sit next beside her.

'Being nice to the pariah?' she asked.

'You're not a pariah.'

'Oh, yes, I am,' she said. 'Most of the people on this ship think I murdered my husband.'

Five

I was so shocked by Blanche's bold statement that it took a minute for me to collect my thoughts before I answered.

'No, they don't,' I said. 'I was told he committed suicide.'

'He did. But "my behavior" caused a lot of suspicion, according to the master. I didn't exactly grieve. So he felt obliged to call the police when we arrived in New York. Just to investigate, he said. According to him, I had opportunity and motive. Opportunity when Eddie's orderly left him alone for a few minutes. Motive because I was a cold fish who didn't take care of my hero husband. They didn't know how plain mean and angry Eddie had become. He didn't want me to touch him, much less care for me. Of course, there was no evidence I'd harmed him, which I hadn't, so I wasn't arrested.'

Blanche flicked her cigarette butt into the sea. A squadron of seabirds following the ship to scavenge our leftovers dived for it, but quickly realized their mistake and turned back to hover over the galley garbage chute.

'So, you were on this ship coming over?'

'Yes, I was. I didn't want to sail back to England on it, but there were so few berths available. I didn't want to wait. Of course, some of the same crew members are on board too – more than

65

enough to tell the story to everyone else. I keep catching people staring at me.'

I didn't know what to say. Blanche wasn't a likeable person, at least under these difficult circumstances, but that didn't mean she was a murderer.

'Your husband was physically able to roll himself off the ship?'

'Oh, yes. He exercised his upper body maniacally. He could lift himself in and out of a chair, the bed and the toilet. He could have easily rolled himself over to the ship's rail, opened the gate and rolled himself right into the sea. And Nigel, Eddie's orderly, told the police he'd been talking a lot about how he didn't want to live the rest of his life in a wheelchair. A few others described what a lousy wife I was.'

'Blanche, all this talk will blow over. Gossip always does. And you're on your way home.'

'Yes, thank God. I wasn't welcomed by Eddie's parents, that's for sure. They were waiting to greet us when the ship docked, with flowers and a welcome banner and everything, only to find out Eddie was dead and the police were questioning me about it. I never spent a night in their home. They gave me enough money for my passage back to England and a hotel room. And they fired Nigel. Which stranded him in a foreign country without a job.'

I could understand why she was bitter. I wanted to advise her that it might help to be a bit more social and likeable to quell the gossip, but decided to keep my mouth shut. I tried another tack.

'Come play hearts with me and Olive,' I said.

Maybe Blanche could relax a bit if she had some company. Olive didn't like her, but I'd bet she'd be kind anyway.

Blanche brushed cigarette ash off her coat. 'No, thanks,' she said. 'I just want to be left alone. I'm going to go back to my bunk and amuse myself by crossing another day off my calendar.'

I stayed on deck for a while, leaning over the rail, watching a school of dolphins follow the ship to pick off the galley trash the seabirds missed, until my hands and feet grew numb.

I almost didn't make it back to my bunk in one piece. As I took the first step on the stairway down to the passengers' quarters, the ship hit a swell and rolled to starboard. I hadn't taken hold of the stair rail yet, and I started to fall. Fortunately, I fell toward the rail and managed to grip it, just banging my knees. Otherwise, I could have fallen all the way down the stairs and been seriously injured.

Grace greeted me at the foot of the stairs. 'Are you all right, ma'am?'

'Yes, I am, thanks. I should have been more careful.'

'Even when the ship seems to be steady, you should never move around it without one hand on a bulkhead or a stair rail.'

I sat on the bottom step and rubbed my knee. I'd ruined my stockings, damn it, and a bruise was already forming. It was a good thing I'd brought some arnica salve with me.

Grace reached down a hand to help me up, and it was then I noticed she had my fur-collared coat

67

over her arm. 'Miss Nunn gave me your coat when I was making her bunk. I told her I was going to your quarters next.' Once inside, she set to making my bunk while I inspected my bedraggled coat.

'I'm afraid it's ruined,' I said. 'I got grease on it this morning.'

'Let me try. I've got some cleaning fluid that might get it out. Anything else you need?'

'I'm fine,' I said. Then I let my curiosity get the better of me.

'Gil told me this morning about Blanche's husband's suicide on their trip over. On this very ship. You were on that voyage too, weren't you?'

Grace neatly tucked my sheets tight, tight enough that a quarter would bounce on them. After she'd arranged the pillows and blankets, she turned to me with a mischievous gleam in her eye. 'I'm not supposed to gossip about the passengers. But you've probably heard most of the story already. Yes, I was on that trip. I was the room steward because of the women on board – an ambassador's wife and her daughter – just as I am now.'

'From what Blanche told me, there are others on our ship that sailed with you, too,' I said.

'Yes. Mr Fox, the man from the American Rubber Company. You've met him. The master and Chief Pitts. And some of the others, you know, like the bosun and the cook. Ensign Bates, but he commanded a different unit. His men this time are all on their first voyage. He's training them, I guess.'

'What about the seamen?' The merchant marine

was a civilian force, now supervised by the Navy, but it still operated much the way it always had. Once a merchant ship docked, the seamen could leave it, but they had to sign on to another ship within three weeks or lose their work card.

'Some of their faces are familiar, but I've been crisscrossing the ocean for two years now and I can't remember who was on what ship.'

'Blanche told me the master called in the police when the *Amelia Earhart* docked in New York.'

'He did. I think regulations required it. Of course, there was no corpse, and no real evidence anyway.'

'Still, it must have been awful for her. Her husband's family rejected her.'

Grace lowered her voice, although no one was nearby to hear her. 'I don't think anyone would have suspected her, except that their marriage was so bad. She spent little time with him. In fact, she slept in a separate berth and played bridge every afternoon in the wardroom. Her husband's orderly picked up all his meals and took them to his room, but she'd eat in the wardroom. And she spent a lot of time with Ensign Bates.'

'With Tom?'

'When he was off watch, they'd smoke on the deck together. Or listen to records in the wardroom. Everyone noticed. It caused a lot of talk.'

I hadn't noticed Tom and Blanche together on this trip, but it wasn't surprising. I supposed they would want to avoid more gossip.

'I've said enough,' Grace said. 'I need to go clean the Smit girls' room. They are not as tidy as you are. I'll take your coat; I'll try that cleaning fluid on it.'

'Thanks.'

After Grace left, humming to herself some jazz tune I couldn't identify, I threw myself on my bunk to wait for the lunch bells. I couldn't help puzzling over everything I'd heard. This was no business of mine, but the OSS had trained me not to accept the obvious, to ask questions and, of course, to keep my mouth shut. I wondered how likely it was that Blanche killed her husband. It seemed that she was looking at being tied to a cripple, and an unlikeable one at that, for the rest of her life. Not a pleasant prospect. People had murdered for much less.

We were allowed to use the wardroom as a lounge when it wasn't mealtime. The seamen used their own mess next door. A cupboard held a record player, records, a stack of well-thumbed books, some games and playing cards. At the end of a watch there was fresh coffee and tea on the server, and sometimes cookies, depending on whether or not the baker had time to fix them.

Olive and I were teaching Corrie and Alida to play hearts. They picked it up quickly and soon we were all slapping cards down and laughing. The girls looked much alike, with blue eyes and blond hair. Corrie's was straight, cut in a chin-length pageboy, but Alida had permed hers and pinned it up in a snood.

Corrie was dealing cards very carefully. Alida, restless as always, tapped the table with a painted fingernail. 'I hate that we're going to England,'

70

she said. 'I wish we could stay in California. It was like heaven there. If I was eighteen, I wouldn't have come. I'd have stayed behind and gotten a job.'

'You can't leave us, Alida!' Corrie said. 'Don't you want to go home?'

'There is no home,' Alida answered. 'The Netherlands is occupied. Nazis are living in our house. England is cold and everyone there is poor and hungry. And bombs fall every night.'

'Can I ask why you're headed to England?' Olive asked.

'Our father has been assigned to the Dutch government in exile,' Alida said. 'He's an economist.'

'I don't think you're supposed to tell,' Corrie said.

'I don't care.'

'Let's play, girls,' I said, changing the subject. 'I have an excellent hand and I want to use it.'

'I wish we had a radio,' Alida said. 'The records in the cabinet are so dull.'

Enough bells rang that I figured the current watch was nearly over. Which meant we needed to vacate the wardroom soon so the messmen could get it ready for dinner. The door swung open and Tom came in.

'You should come up on deck,' he said to us. 'We're in the Gulf Stream now and the weather is beautiful. It won't last long.' He closed the door behind him.

'That ensign is the only decent-looking man on this ship,' Alida said.

* * *

71

The entire ship's crew, except for those on watch, gathered on deck to enjoy the sunshine. Several seamen tossed a football about while a few just lay flat on their backs on the deck to soak up the sun. A group of four threw dice furtively. Even the master and Popeye were outside, leaning on the rail of the bridge deck, smoking their pipes. Seabirds careened around us, squawking. It was lovely and warm, and I unbuttoned my peacoat and pulled off my watch cap.

For the first time I could see the ships sailing with us. I was no expert but I guessed they were two oil tankers, three more Liberty cargo ships and another large ship that looked like a cruise ship converted for troop transport. This motley fleet was protected by three corvettes, which didn't look large enough to defend a fleet of fishing boats. Surely at least one destroyer would join us in Halifax for our voyage across the Atlantic!

Olive appeared on deck and we joined arms to stroll around the perimeter of the ship, probably the most exercise I'd had since coming aboard. We took our time, stopping to look out to sea, hoping to see dolphins or even sharks following us.

As we approached the afterdeck, we had to squeeze between two ambulances to stay on our course. We found ourselves in a secluded space between several jeeps. Tom and Blanche were lounging in one of the jeeps, well out of sight of most of the deck. We interrupted Tom in the act of lighting Blanche's cigarette. They didn't look as if they'd been necking or anything, but they didn't seem pleased to see us either. But they collected themselves. Tom said, 'We're taking some time away from the crowd. Would you like to join us?' He gestured to the back seat of the jeep.

'We're solving a number of world problems,' Blanche said, drawing on her cigarette. 'You can help us.' To their relief, we turned down their invitation.

'We're getting some exercise,' I said.

'Good idea,' Tom said. 'The weather will turn nasty again by tonight, when we pass New York City and turn north.'

Olive and I kept walking and managed to hold back our giggles until we were out of earshot. Then we turned into teenagers.

'Do you believe that!' Olive said. 'What does that nice young officer see in Blanche?'

'She's an attractive woman,' I said. 'Besides, we don't know if they were canoodling.'

'Please! Don't insult me.'

Then I told Olive that Blanche and Tom already knew each other. I figured it was OK since it wasn't a secret that they'd sailed together on the *Amelia Earhart* on its voyage from England to the States when Blanche's husband died. Finding them alone together raised all kinds of tantalizing questions without answers, but there was no evidence that the two of them had more than an acquaintance, and I didn't want to be the person who spread gossip about them. Enough people on this ship already believed Blanche had murdered her husband.

* * *

73

The sound of multiple foghorns woke me early the next morning. And it was frigid again. I'd let a foot stick out from my covers overnight; I massaged it to bring back a little warmth and hoped it hadn't developed frostbite. It was still some time before I could take my bath. No way was I going to get out of bed before then!

More ships must have joined our little parade as I heard many more foghorns than the previous day. We'd passed New York City and left the Gulf Stream overnight. Foghorns were far and away the worst sound I'd ever heard – I grew up with them, and the best description I ever had was an out-of-tune tuba. A constant, ear-splitting racket, but better than crashing into another ship. During the war, radio activity was kept to an absolute minimum. It was a relief not to hear the news every day.

The fog lifted once the sun came out and after breakfast all of us casual passengers went out on deck to watch our approach to Halifax. The idea of going into town energized us. We'd only been at sea for a few days but we were eager to escape our close quarters. Once we departed Halifax, we'd be at sea for several weeks. After breakfast we gathered at a table in the wardroom and laid our plans.

'I going to find an Irish pub near the port,' Ronan said, his voice muffled by the scarf wrapped around his face. 'I need a pint – no, two pints – of Guinness in the worst way. And it must have a fire in the lounge. A big fire.'

'I know just the place. I spent a few days here waiting for transport the last time I sailed from the States,' Gil said. 'It's called the Galway, and it was well stocked with whisky. It had a wonderful rabbit pie and chips, too.'

Mr Smit looked at his wife, as if asking for permission to join the men.

'You go on ahead, *Beste*; we'll join you later,' she said. 'The girls and I will be looking for a tea parlor. We want a fireplace too!'

'Maybe they'll have croissants,' Corrie said. 'With jam.'

'I wonder where the officers go when they're ashore,' Alida mused.

Smit fixed his elder daughter with a steely gaze. 'You stay with your mother and sister,' he said. 'No arguments.'

'You'd think I was a child!' she exclaimed.

'You are a child,' he answered her. Alida sulked, looking out to sea with her bottom lip stuck out and her arms crossed.

'I'm going to find a bookstore,' Olive said. 'I've read the book I brought already. Have you seen what's in the so-called ship's library? Westerns! Zane Grey and Hopalong Cassidy! Why do the seamen read so many Westerns? I'll bet none of them have ever been on a horse in their lives!'

My only goal was to buy a couple of pairs of wool socks and wool mittens.

Olive and I agreed, depending on how long we could stay ashore, to join the men at the pub for a meal of rabbit pie and chips after our various excursions. You would think we were going to Paris, we were so excited.

The master, who was sitting at another table

with Ensign Bates and his second mate, must have heard part of our conversation. He rose and came over to our table.

'Would you mind if I join you?' he asked.

'Of course not,' Gil said.

The master pulled out a chair, turned it around, and sat with his arms crossed over the back. 'I couldn't help but overhear you,' he said.

'What time will you be allowing us to go ashore?' Alida asked.

'I'm sorry to disappoint you,' he said. 'But no one will be going ashore in Halifax except me and several of my officers.'

I'm sure surprise and disappointment showed on all our faces. Poor Mrs Smit actually covered her face with her hands. Ronan looked as if he'd lost his best friend. He would have to wait weeks longer for that pint. I had hardly taken off my kid gloves since I'd gotten on this ship and now I didn't expect to. They were already ruined by salt spray. I'd need to throw them away once I arrived in England.

Gil was furious. 'You can't keep us from going ashore!' he said. 'There's no reason!'

'Yes, I can,' the master said. 'And I don't have to explain why. But I will. Halifax isn't safe for tourists, or for shore leave for our seamen, for that matter. The port is overwhelmed. It can't handle the troops, ships or workers it already has. If you did go ashore, you'd never get into a restaurant or a pub. And it's dangerous – the city is packed with the kind of people who prey on tourists and seamen on shore leave. Even the harbor's full; we can't even drop anchor there.'

'You're going ashore, dammit,' Gil said, under his breath.

'Yes, I am. Chief Pitts, Ensign Bates and I have to fill out forms at the port and the chief steward is going to stock up on supplies, if he can find any.'

The Smits had gone below, so Olive, Gil, Ronan and I went out on deck, but not before hearing from a seaman going off watch that it was seven degrees above zero outside. We knocked ice off the rails before grabbing them to hang on as the ship maneuvered near the shore. The coastline looked empty, cold and bleak. From a distance, the town of Halifax was gray and industrial-looking, consisting mostly of warehouses, cranes, piers and a harbor packed with all kinds of ships, from destroyers to cruise liners confiscated by the government for troop transport. The others went below while our ship cruised to an inlet to drop anchor. I stayed for a few minutes to watch a brightly lit freight train chug around the inlet, its whistle making that familiar lonesome, home-sick sound. Occasionally, it would stop, its whistle sounding in a long burst, to pick up cargo or passengers to take to the port, where long-shoremen would empty its freight cars and load them on waiting ships.

On my way back amidships, I saw Grace and a seaman smoking, sitting on one of the many wooden cable spools that were scattered around the deck, which Olive had started to call 'the deck chairs'. The seaman was the young red-headed man I'd seen boarding the ship at the last minute at the Navy Yard. When he saw me, he tossed his still-glowing cigarette into the ocean and rapidly walked away, his head down. I guessed he wasn't supposed to be there. I didn't blame him; Grace was such a pretty girl. She moved aside to give me room.

'Cigarette?' she asked me, holding out her pack and Zippo lighter.

'No, thanks,' I said. 'Smoking makes my throat sore.'

She nodded, looking toward the Nova Scotia shore while inhaling a deep lungful of smoke.

'Just three weeks until we get to England,' she said. 'I love it there.'

'Really?' I said, surprised. 'Even with the bombing and rationing? Have you spent much time there?' I was so looking forward to living in London, despite the crushing work that awaited me, not to mention the deprivations and bombings. I'd wanted to go to Europe ever since I could remember and this was likely my only chance.

'I had a three-week layover in Liverpool – you know, in between ships. It was like a different world.'

I knew what she meant. England wasn't segregated.

She tossed her spent cigarette overboard and jammed her hands into her pockets.

'I would love to live there after the war. I guess I'm not much of a patriot,' she said. 'Are you terribly shocked?'

'Not at all,' I said. 'I would think the same way if I were you.' Madeleine, Dellaphine's daughter,

78

had said many times that she wanted to live in Paris after the war, where she could be as free as Josephine Baker. Her mother scoffed at the idea. To Dellaphine, it sounded like a fairy tale. 'You know,' I said to Grace, 'you can talk to me about anything. I'm on your side.'

I had given up any tolerance of segregation, despite my upbringing, after I moved to DC. Washington was teeming with people from all over the country, all over the world. I'd seen things I never knew existed. Like men dancing together and holding hands at a private party. One of my white colleagues was engaged to a beautiful mixed-race woman from the Caribbean. And one of the academic experts in the Research Section of OSS was a woman with a PhD. She lived with another woman in a 'Boston marriage'. Madeleine had graduated from the best colored high school in the city and had a good job with the Social Security Administration.

From what I'd seen, colored people could do anything white people could do, and why shouldn't they keep right on doing it?

'When I was in Liverpool, I was quartered in a women's boarding house,' Grace said. 'The landlady was so nice. It wasn't just colored – there was an Indian lady, and the other three were white ladies who worked at the port. They were all from London. The Indian lady let me try on her saris – they were beautiful. We all ate dinner together and everything. We could go into any tea shop and order tea and scones whenever we wanted to. And sit with the audience at the cinema instead of in a balcony.'

I said nothing to discourage her. Eleanor Roosevelt was leading a movement for equal rights for colored people, but it would be a long struggle. Grace stood up to go. 'Mrs Pearlie, you won't tell anyone what I said, will you? About leaving the United States.'

'Of course not,' I said.

Talking to Grace made me wonder how the world would sort itself out after the war. It seemed very unlikely to me that things would go back to the way they were, as Phoebe and Henry had insisted nostalgically.

I joined Gil, Ronan and Olive in the gangway down below, where we chatted, putting off returning to our berths where there was nothing to do except lie on our bunks and try to stay warm. The next three weeks promised to be just as cold and bleak as this day. I already had cabin fever and I couldn't for the life of me think of how we'd all pass the time ahead of us.

'Look,' Gil said, 'I've got two bottles of Four Roses bourbon. I'm happy to share it. And a deck of cards. Can everyone play poker? Let's have a poker party after dinner.'

'I'm in,' I said, 'I've got a pint of gin.'

We agreed to meet after dinner in Ronan's cabin for drinks and cards. The plan lifted all our spirits. You'd think we'd been invited to the party of the century!

The shore party must have returned because we saw the master, Tom and Popeye at the officers' table at dinner.

Olive and I were fed up with Blanche. So her husband was dead – lots of women had dead husbands and they didn't sit by themselves at dinner rather than taking a spot at a table with people who were willing to be nice to her. Me, for example. So Olive and I marched up to her table, where she was sitting by herself as usual, and plunked our trays right down. This did not improve Blanche's demeanor.

'Sitting with the suspected murderess?' she said to us. 'Is this your good deed for the day?'

'People might not think you're a murderess if you acted like a human being sometimes,' Olive said to her.

To our surprise Blanche smiled. 'I know,' she said. 'But it's so difficult. Everyone on this ship has heard about Eddie's death and how I was a lousy wife and maybe even killed him. I just want to hide until I get home.'

'You can't hide here. There's not enough room,' I said. 'Might as well mingle and try to have some fun. And I know how annoying it is to hear that. I'm a widow, too.'

'You are socializing a bit, though, aren't you?' Olive said, winking at Blanche.

'It's not what you think. Tom and I are friends. On the voyage over, when Eddie died, he was the only person who was nice to me.'

Dinner was pretty good. We had sliced turkey and gravy – real turkey, not canned – the usual mashed potatoes, green beans and fresh baked rolls. Butter instead of margarine. Chocolate pudding for dessert. There were always bowls of

81

apples on the table so you could take one for a snack later. I figured about ten days from now our meals would be less appetizing as the cooks switched to powdered eggs, powdered milk and margarine.

The three of us avoided serious subjects and talked about the movies we'd seen and the books we were reading. Like me, Blanche was an Agatha Christie fan. She said she had an entire shelf devoted to her books in her room at her parents' home in Winchester and had *Evil Under the Sun* autographed when Mrs Christie was at Harrod's once. Her favorite was *Death on the Nile*, but mine was *The Murder of Roger Ackroyd*. To our surprise, Olive had read all the Agatha Christie books, too. For some reason we had thought she was too serious to waste her time on detective fiction.

While we waited for a messman to clear off our table, I noticed that Blanche wrapped up her dinner roll, which she had left on her plate, in a napkin and stowed it in her purse. Then she leaned across the table and took two apples out of the bowl of fruit on the table.

'I get hungry at bedtime,' she said, noticing our stares. 'There's so much time between dinner and breakfast.'

After we'd finished coffee and dessert, the master stood up from his chair and rapped on the table. We quieted, eager to hear what he had to say.

'As you know,' he said, 'my officers and I went to Halifax today to verify our orders. We were told that most of the ships we've been

82

traveling with will part from us tomorrow and join a fast convey. It'll head north to resupply Iceland before it arrives in England. We'll connect with a slow convoy in St John's and take the direct route to England. We'll be traveling at a speed of seven knots and we should reach Liverpool in nineteen days. We'll have air cover and warship escorts the entire way, but I want you to understand that this is still a dangerous journey. Most of the German submarine activity takes place off the west coast of the British Isles these days, but lone wolves still surface often in the center of convoys. And as I am sure you have noticed, the weather is nasty, and it will be worse on the open ocean. Once we leave St John's, you must wear your life jackets at all times, day and night. No exceptions. Any questions?'

He was met with silence.

'All right,' he said. 'You may go.'

I was pushing my chair to the table, preparing to leave, when Tom came up to me. He handed me a paper bag. 'This is for you,' he said, looking a little embarrassed. 'Blanche said you were pretty desperate for these.'

To my joy, I pulled out thick wool mittens and two pairs of wool socks and clutched them to my chest. 'Thank you! I don't know what to say!' I turned to Blanche. 'I didn't think to ask anyone to look for these. Thank you!' Blanche just shrugged, looking embarrassed.

'I was lucky,' Tom said. 'The stores are almost empty. But I ducked under an awning to avoid a gust of snow and saw these in the display window. They would only sell me two pairs of socks and I got the last of the mittens.'

Ronan's room was a double berth, which meant there was a second bunk above the first and a little more floor space than in the single berths. Olive and I sat cross-legged on the bottom bunk. Gil and Ronan got their suitcases from the storage closet and upended them, using them as stools.

I'd brought my pint of Gordon's gin with me and some of Dellaphine's pralines. Olive donated a can of peanuts and Ronan a bag of potato chips – or, as he called them, crisps. True to his word, Gil produced a bottle of Four Roses. No one wanted to drink gin straight but me. Which was just fine: my bottle would last longer.

Because of the master's warnings, we weren't the gayest group ever, but it was better than being alone in our cabins. We parceled the snacks out on paper napkins and poured our drinks into glasses borrowed from the wardroom.

'These pralines are delicious,' Olive said.

'The cook at my boarding house, Dellaphine, made them.' I was instantly awash with memories of my two years in Washington. The good ones. My new friends, my lover Joe and my work. And making my own living. That was the best part. I hoped that after the war I could continue to do that. Like most government girls, I was employed for the duration of the war. I could be out of a job within days of the Allied victory and unable to find a new one, since men leaving the military would get preference for the jobs that were available. That's just the way it was. Women were expendable. They could always go back to keeping house. Which meant I might need to return to my parents' home to live. And work in the family fish camp, frying up bluefish and hushpuppies. I gulped down half my glass of gin. I wished I had an ice cube or two, but when I tasted the gin it was as cold as it could be without being frozen solid. It quickly worked its way through my body until I felt almost warm. And less worried. I would do my best to find a job with some permanence before the end of the war. And a woman friend of mine at OSS, who was a college professor at Smith before the war, had said she would help me finish college if I wanted.

And how could I complain when so many European women had lost their homes, livelihoods and loved ones? The fate of the Jews of Europe was catastrophic, and rumors abounded that millions had been executed in concentration camps. I remembered my dear friend Rachel Bloch, a French Jewish woman I'd met in junior college. She'd just barely escaped France to Malta with her children after her husband joined the French Resistance. I liked to think I had something to do with that, although I didn't know for sure.

I should be ashamed of myself for whining. Instead, I thought about my future. My plan was to have a good job, my own apartment and a car. Maybe that was as much a fairy tale as Grace's desire to live in England, but I was going to work as hard as I could to make it come true.

85

Ronan finished his glass of Gil's bourbon and smacked his lips. 'That's good stuff,' he said. 'Even if it's not Irish.'

Olive took a sip of her bourbon cautiously, then another. 'I usually don't drink anything but sherry.' She swallowed another mouthful. 'This isn't as sweet as sherry. It's kind of raw. I like it.'

'So,' Ronan said to her, 'you're a nurse? What kind of nursing do you do?'

'Surgical. I assist surgeons during operations.'

'Really,' Ronan said, looking surprised. 'That's class. Why didn't you tell us earlier?'

Olive shrugged. 'I've learned not to mention it. Surgery makes people squeamish. And there are still people who think women don't belong in an operating theatre at all.'

'What about you?' I said to Gil. 'You said you work for a rubber company?'

'The American Rubber Company. We make tires for airplanes. Our factory has quadrupled its production since the war started; we can hardly find enough workers to fill our contracts, even with half of our workforce women. I'm going to England to sign a new contract. This is my third trip in two years.'

We finished our snacks and refilled our drinks. 'If we're going to play poker, we should do it now, before we get too soused to think,' Gil said. He reached into his coat pocket and pulled out a deck of cards. 'What shall we play for?' he asked. 'Nickels? Dimes? More than that?'

'Oh, no,' Olive said, 'I'm not playing for money. I work too hard to waste my pay gambling.'

'How about just pennies?' Gil said. 'It's no fun if you don't bet real money!'

'I can't afford to lose money gambling,' Ronan said. 'I'm a poor man. I'll probably spend my last penny the morning before I die in the afternoon.'

I was relieved. I didn't want to play for money either. 'Louise,' Ronan said, 'I've got a big box of matches in that drawer there – can you reach it?'

I could, and pulled the red, white and blue box of Victory matches out and handed it over to him. He divvied them up between us. Gil wasn't pleased, but he shuffled the deck anyway.

'Draw poker, deuces wild, OK?' he asked.

'That's all I know how to play,' Olive said.

Olive and I sat cross-legged on the bunk facing each other. Gil and Ronan perched on their upended suitcases. Gil dealt into the space on the bunk between Olive and me. I had a miserable hand, even more miserable after I discarded three cards and drew three more. Ronan and Olive folded soon after I did.

So Gil won the first hand with a pair of jacks. Not surprising. He obviously had played many times. He scooped the little pot of matchsticks into his own pile.

My next hand was a little better. I had four clubs, not in sequence, and the king of hearts. OK. So if I discarded the king and drew another club, I'd have a flush. Unfortunately, I drew the eight of hearts and wound up with nothing. So I folded. So did Olive. Ronan appeared to have a good hand and kept tossing matchsticks into the pot, vying with Gil. But when Ronan slapped down his pair of tens, Gil trumped him with two queens and two threes.

Gil's stack of matches grew while ours shrank. More disturbing to me, though, was that Gil seemed to revel in winning. There was a triumphant gleam in his eye when he threw his winning hands down. The others didn't seem to notice, but I didn't like it. So I watched him shuffle and deal, which he did very quickly and competently. I didn't like the placement of the little finger on his right hand directly under the deck.

Sure enough, Gil won the next hand, too. This time with just a pair of eights, but Ronan, Olive and I had nothing. It occurred to me that I hadn't seen a single ace yet. And the deck of cards was his; he'd taken it out of his coat pocket at the beginning of the game.

'Let me shuffle and deal,' I said. 'I'd like to practice.' Gil had no choice but to hand the deck over to me. I carefully and completely shuffled the cards and dealt them out. In my hand were two aces. I discarded three cards and drew three, one of which was a two of hearts. I had three of a kind – the winning hand. I scooped up the pot and for just a second I met Gil's eyes. I wouldn't say he looked guilty – it was more like anger I saw there – but I knew he'd been cheating, and he knew I knew. He'd stacked the deck and dealt from the bottom. For a game with friends over matches.

I didn't say anything to the others. We all had to live on this ship for another three dangerous weeks and I didn't want to introduce any dissension. But I filed away the pure fact that Gilbert Fox couldn't be trusted.

Six

Our convoy's departure from the St John's Harbor was quite a spectacle. For the first time since leaving DC, the sky was clear and blue. A brass band on one of the docks played 'Yankee Doodle Dandy', while a crowd that had gathered on the shore cheered, waving Canadian and American flags and throwing their hats high.

Two fighter planes zoomed out to sea to scout for German submarines that might be lying in wait, while a US Navy blimp shadowed us overhead, its metal skin gleaming in the sun. So many chunks of ice floated in the ocean that it gave us the feeling we were plowing through snow. A flock of seabirds flew overhead, making a raucous noise, waiting for our ships to jettison their garbage once the convoy was well out of the harbor.

We casual passengers, bundled up in the usual coats, hats, scarves and gloves, and wearing our life preservers, lined the *Amelia Earhart*'s rail, trying to count the number of ships in our convoy. We settled on perhaps forty, including seven corvettes, two escort destroyers and a sloop, the *Robin*. Escort destroyers were smaller and slower than fleet destroyers because the convoys, and their prey, German submarines, were slow. They had fewer torpedoes and guns than fleet destroyers, but a heavy anti-submarine battery.

The *Robin* was a Royal Navy vessel and much faster than our other escorts. It could travel at sixteen knots.

The Brits had trouble naming their vessels, too; there just weren't enough halfway famous dead people. So the sloops were named after birds and the corvettes after flowers. One of our corvettes was *Daisy*, another *Violet*. Not terribly warlike!

One of the two escort destroyers, the *Evans*, was the convoy commodore ship, which meant it was the flagship for the convoy commander. The *Evans* had a corvette painted on the side as camouflage. We sailed near it since our cargo, all those munitions, needed the most protection. The second destroyer was the *Lawrence*, which I couldn't see. It flanked the convoy miles behind us.

I was grateful for all our escorts, but, honestly, the corvettes were surprisingly small – not much bigger than the Coast Guard patrol boats I was used to seeing on the North Carolina coast. It was hard to imagine that one could take on a submarine.

'Look at that,' Alida said, pointing out to an ocean liner, painted gray and converted to a troop-ship, that steamed along behind us. 'Do you think it's the *Queen Mary*?'

'I doubt it,' I said. 'It's too small. And the *Queen Mary* is much faster than this convoy.' I'd heard the Grey Ghost was so swift she often steamed alone and unprotected across the Atlantic.

Most of the cargo ships in our convoy were either Liberty ships or the newer Victory ships, packed until they were low in the water. Food, vehicle parts, fuel, airplanes, jeeps, troops, even mules. Not just supplies for England any more, but provisions for an invasion. The Allies were going to attack the German occupiers of Fortress Europe at last, with everything they had. Please God, let it be enough!

As we steamed out to sea, the passengers slowly drifted away from the rail, motivated by the freezing cold and Grace's announcement that coffee and cocoa were available in the wardroom. Until just Olive and I stood together.

'Well,' Olive said, 'we're on our way. There's no turning back now.'

I'd had the same thought. The next land we saw would be Northern Ireland. In three weeks.

Seven

We knew there was a storm coming. We'd been on the open sea for a week. Fog and heavy clouds surrounded us again. The convoy ships' foghorns sounded endlessly. One night I thought of stuffing my ears with cotton to block out the sound but then realized I might miss the siren to run for the lifeboats. The ocean's swells were deep and choppy waves smacked our hull, sending Mrs Smit to her bed with seasickness. Grace doled out peppermint candy and ginger, which she seemed to possess in endless supply, and Olive and I chewed ginger constantly to keep our stomachs settled. Reading was out of the question. We passed the days playing hearts and gin rummy with the Smit girls. Blanche taught us all how to play cribbage with a set she'd brought with her. We danced to records on the record player set up in the wardroom.

On the third morning I awoke to even rougher seas. I decided to take a sponge bath instead of submerging myself naked in the bathtub. I dressed quickly and joined the others in the mess line. The chalkboard menu announced that for the duration of the voyage fresh eggs would be rationed. One per person every other day. This was not an egg day. We had pancakes with margarine and table syrup.

We saw Sparky in the mess and asked him

about the weather forecast, even though we knew he wasn't supposed to tell us. And he didn't, but his expression told us it wasn't good. The master and Chief Popeye in the wardroom didn't seem particularly worried, but they were sitting alone having an intense conversation.

Olive, Gil and Ronan went outside to smoke. I joined them for some fresh air.

Clearly the ship was in 'all hands on deck' mode. The deck crawled with seamen, including oilers and wipers from the engine room. All the cables holding down the vehicles were tested. The 'deck chairs' – the empty wooden cable spools – were tied to the railings. Loose equipment was stowed away. Gunners stationed at all the guns were securing them, under Tom's direction. When I looked up at the bridge deck, I could see the master and four other people, all with their eyes on the sky.

When we went back to our quarters, we met Grace in the gangway. She confirmed what we already knew. 'There's a gale on the way,' she said. 'Dress in as many clothes as you can. Do not take off your life vest for any reason. Make sure all your gear is stowed away. You don't want to be smacked in the head by a flying hairbrush or cologne bottle.'

Lunch was cold sandwiches, fruit and cookies. The seamen ate quickly, stuffing cookies and fruit into the pockets of their foul-weather gear before going back to their chores. Smit packed enough food for his wife and daughters into a bag to take back to their cabin. I ate little – half a sandwich, and that was only because I knew

93

I needed something in my stomach. Olive left half of her sandwich, too.

'If you're not going to finish those, can I have them?' Blanche asked.

The woman must have had a tapeworm. 'Sure,' I said, pushing my plate over to her.

'You want mine, too?' Olive asked.

Blanche took both our sandwich halves and the cookies donated by Ronan, wrapped them in her handkerchief and stuffed them in her pocketbook. 'Just in case I want to eat dinner in my bunk,' she said. 'Walking around the ship could be pretty treacherous in a few hours.'

As if to warn us all, a huge swell hit the ship, tilting the floor of the wardroom sharply.

Ronan grabbed me by the arm or I would have fallen. Gil, who was on the downside of the tilt, blocked dishes and cutlery from crashing off the table. The ship righted itself and a couple of messmen scurried about clearing the tables and picking up what had fallen on the floor.

'Anyone want to go outside and get a last breath of fresh air and a smoke with me?' Gil asked.

'I'll come,' Ronan said, feeling in his pocket for his pipe. 'Just for a minute.'

'I think the place for me is my bunk,' I said. 'Until this passes.' Olive and Blanche agreed. So the three of us struggled back to our berths. We used both hands to fend off the bulkheads as we worked our way down our staircase to the passenger quarters. When Olive and I reached the bottom, we caught our breath, hanging on to the staircase rail. Blanche wasn't behind us.

'Where does that woman go?' Olive said.

'Perhaps she's meeting Tom somewhere,' I answered.

'That can't be it. All the officers are on duty. He'll be on deck.'

Ronan clattered down the stairs, holding on to the rail with both hands. He was soaking wet. 'It's impossible outside,' he said. 'We stood inside the door to the deck and still couldn't light up. Master passed by and ordered all of us to stay in our berths until the storm passes.'

'Wants us out of the way, and I'm happy to oblige him,' said Gil, who'd followed Ronan down the stairs.

Another huge wave struck the ship. The four of us were flung up against the interior bulkhead, grabbing at anything we could to keep our footing. Only Gil managed to stay upright; he'd gotten hold of one of the bars riveted to the bulkhead and clung on to it with both hands.

'Holy Mother of God,' Ronan said. 'It's times like this I hope welding holds as well as rivets.'

The ship shifted back to a level pitch, but who knew how long that would last. Ronan helped Olive and me to our feet. 'I wish I had two life jackets,' Olive said. 'I'd wrap another one around my waist.'

'Speaking of two life jackets,' Ronan said, 'did one of you take the second one out of my berth?'

'What are you talking about?' Gil said.

'I had a second one in my berth because it's a double bunk. I went to get it in case someone else needed it, but it was gone.'

'One of the stewards took it, I'll bet,' I said.

95

'They'd know you had two; they might want some extras on hand in a storm like this.'

We felt the ship begin to pitch again and all headed straight to our berths.

'Time to batten down the hatches,' Olive shouted, as she closed her door.

I slammed my door and climbed into my bunk, hanging on to the grab bar welded to the head of my bunk. I wondered where on earth Blanche was. What a strange woman! But wherever she was hunkered down, she was going to have to fend for herself; it was all the rest of us could do to take care of ourselves.

Eight

No one went to dinner. The ship was pitching and rolling so much that it would be worth your life to try to walk around. The thought of eating was nauseating anyway. I kept my bucket in the bunk with me until I had nothing left in my stomach to barf up. Only by gripping the grab bar with both hands could I prevent myself from being thrown out of bed.

Waves and rain pounded my little porthole over and over again. The ship creaked until I was sure the rumors about her lousy construction were true and she was breaking apart. I could hear foghorns blaring as the ships in the convoy tried to keep from crashing into each other. I thought I could hear the Smit girls crying and occasionally an Irish curse from Ronan. I screamed myself several times, the loudest when I swear the ship was standing on end.

I heard the bells for the watch change at six in the morning and the sound of feet overhead. The storm was abating, thank God. My heart was pounding and I had sweated through my heavy clothing.

Before long I felt I could stand up, though I was dizzy when I did. I changed into dry clothes, shivering with cold. After buttoning up my peacoat, pulling on my watch cap and buckling my life preserver, I went to my door and opened it.

'Is everyone OK?' I called out. Ronan opened his door. Gil followed. He had a bruise forming on his forehead. 'Are you all right?' I asked.

'Damn grab bar pulled loose from the bulkhead and I banged my head. I'm fine,' he said.

I went down the hall, still bouncing off the bulkheads, and knocked on the Smits' door.

Mrs Smit opened the door. 'We are fine,' she said in her heavy Dutch accent. 'But hungry. The girls are getting dressed to go to breakfast.' We were all hungry now that the ship was on a stable keel. Most of us had missed dinner.

Olive met me in the passageway. 'Blanche still isn't in her room, the dope. Where do you think she is?' she said.

'We'll find out soon enough, I guess,' I said. I was losing patience with Blanche. We all had enough to worry about without babysitting her.

Blanche was in the wardroom, calm as she could be, eating cornflakes and canned fruit from the cold breakfast that had been set out for us.

'I'm sorry,' she said, before Olive and I had a chance to reprimand her. 'I waited a second too long on deck and couldn't make it to my berth without risking injury. I spent the storm in a utility closet – very uncomfortable it was, too. I hope you weren't worried.'

'Of course we were,' I said, setting down my tray. Olive didn't join us; she was too annoyed with Blanche. She took her tray and went to sit with the Smits, Ronan and Gil.

98

'Well, don't be. I can take care of myself.'

'None of us can take care of ourselves completely. We all need help sometimes.'

She didn't answer me. We finished breakfast in silence.

All hands were on deck. Seamen rushed through the breakfast line, ate standing up and returned to their posts as soon as they were done. Some were wearing soaked foul-weather gear, which must have meant they were on deck during the gale. I couldn't imagine it.

All of us passengers trooped outside, swathed in the usual layers of sweaters, coats, scarves and mittens. The gale was well past us, but it was still freezing outside. Otherwise, the sea was calm and even the sun shone occasionally through white clouds. The smokers in our crowd lit their cigarettes immediately and Ronan lit his pipe while the Smits and I watched the chaos on deck.

Despite the frenetic preparations for the gale, ropes, cables, electrical cords, pieces of tarp and unidentifiable – to me, anyway – detritus littered the deck. Seamen pushed water off the side of the ship with wide brooms and mops. Others secured vehicle cables that had slipped off the cargo. Tom and the gunners removed the tarps protecting the artillery and checked the guns by firing them in short bursts.

We were shocked to see an ambulance hanging by one cable off the side of the ship. The master, Popeye and the chief engineer were talking about what to do while a group of seamen waited for instructions.

'We should cut it loose, sir,' the engineer said. 'It's just one vehicle.'

'But it's an ambulance, not just another jeep,' Popeye said. 'Our boys will need it.'

'What's likely to happen if we try to retrieve it?' the master asked.

'We could damage the ship,' the engineer said. 'Dragging it up the side of the ship over the rail could tear up the railing and part of the hull. It's not worth it.'

'Can't we use a winch?'

'Not at sea. Not safely, anyway. Without the ship secured in a dock, the winch might not hold,' he said.

'All right,' the master said. 'Cut the ambulance loose, damn it.'

'Master, sir,' Tom said, appearing by the master's side.

'Yes?'

'The commodore destroyer is signaling us. Permission to answer, sir.'

'Granted,' the master said. 'How many signalmen do you have?'

'Two, sir.'

'Set them both up. One to communicate with the *Evans*, one to communicate with the convoy.'

'Yes, sir.'

If there was still a convoy. Fortunately, we were still near the *Evans*, but I saw few of our companion ships nearby. They were bound to have been scattered by the storm. And I knew that radio contact would continue to be minimal. It made sense that German submarines, knowing that the convoy was disorganized, might be nearby, waiting for an opportunity to sink as many of our cargo ships as they could.

'Master,' a seaman said, approaching while the master watched a couple of seamen with blow-torches cut through the cable which dangled the ambulance over the edge of the ship.

'Yes.'

'The chief engineer needs you to see something.'

'OK,' the master said, turning to follow him. No one was paying a whit of attention to Olive or me, so we trailed behind him, curious. We came upon a group examining a rent in the deck aft, several feet long, big enough for us to gasp.

'Goddamn welds!' the master cursed, ignoring the rule against swearing in front of women. 'Goddammit! How bad is it?'

'We can repair it,' the engineer said. 'But if it keeps tearing . . .' He shook his head.

'How will you repair it?' the master asked.

'Sheet metal to cover it,' the chief engineer said. 'All tied together with metal straps and bolts. But there's another thing.'

'What now?'

'We'll need to inspect the skin of the entire ship. Inside and out. There could be more.'

'All right. Do it.'

Tom appeared at the master's side again. 'Sir,' he said, 'the commodore ship is sending a launch with the *Evans*' executive officer to confer with you.'

'Good.'

'It's on its way.'

'Winch down the accommodation staircase and I'll be right there.'

During the pause that followed, I gathered the courage to speak to the master.

'Sir,' I said. The master turned around and seemed surprised to see Olive and me standing there.

'You should be below,' he said. 'You're in the way on deck.'

'We'd like to help,' Olive said. 'With something. Something useful.'

'Anything,' I said. I'd felt useless watching the officers and seamen struggling to get the ship back in operation. I wasn't used to standing around watching other people labor when there was plenty of work to go around.

'You know,' he said. 'You can help. We've got several injured men. This is the pharmacist's mate's first cruise. I doubt he knows what to do.'

'I'll go get my medical bag,' Olive said.

'The injured men are in the first-aid room,' the master said.

'I know where it is,' I said to Olive. 'I'll meet you there.'

When I got to the first-aid room, I found several battered men outside in the hall waiting to be seen, including one with a horrendous black eye.

'I hope you're here to help us, ma'am,' he said to me. 'I don't think that pharmacist's mate knows what he's doing. He's really hurting the guy in there.'

I heard a yelp from inside the first-aid room, just as Olive appeared in the corridor with her medical bag. The injured men seemed quite

102

relieved to see her. She looked like one of the army nurses in a recruitment poster, radiating determination and confidence. She knocked on the door and went in without an answer. 'I'll get you an ice pack for that eye,' I said to the seaman with the black eye. 'It looks awful.'

'It hurts like anything, ma'am,' he said.

Inside the first-aid room I found Olive reprimanding the pharmacist's mate, whose surname was Isted. 'You cannot treat a man with a burn that severe without a painkiller,' she said. 'It's cruel.'

The injured man's wound was ghastly. I guessed it was second degree – bright red, swollen and already blistering. It covered a large part of his forearm and the palm of his hand.

'But, ma'am,' Isted said, 'protocol is that I examine and clean the wound first.'

'Nuts to that,' she said. 'Is there any morphine in the medicine chest?'

Isted handed over the chest and Olive found a syringe and a vial of morphine. 'Here we go; you'll feel better in a few minutes,' she said to the injured man. 'What's your name? How did this happen?'

The man was a wiper from the engine room. He was soaked with sweat and oil. He and his fellow wipers and oilers had spent hours furiously working to keep the engine functioning during the gale. 'I'm Ordinary Seaman Price,' he said. 'I tripped and fell on to the boiler. It hurts so much!'

Olive expertly drew out morphine from the vial with the syringe and injected him. She turned to the pharmacist's mate.

'Isted,' she said, 'when a man is this pale and shaky, he is probably in shock. He needs to lie down and elevate his legs.' The two of them helped the injured man recline while I located some pillows. 'Would you please clean the oil away from the burn with alcohol,' she asked the pharmacist's mate. 'Don't touch the wound itself. We'll wait until the morphine kicks in to dress it.'

'Ma'am,' Isted said, 'you just tell me what you want me to do and I will do it.'

'Olive, I need an ice pack for a seaman with a black eye,' I said.

'Let me get it for you,' Isted said, opening a cabinet and pulling out an ice pack and filling it with ice from a small freezer.

'Make sure you wrap that in a cloth of some kind,' Olive said to him. 'Otherwise, it could be too cold and damage the tissue. Louise, can you triage the others in the hall, too?'

'I'll do my best.'

Isted gazed at Olive as though he was in the presence of a goddess. I figured his education was little more than a couple of weeks' worth of basic first aid and he could see that Olive knew what she was doing.

Out in the passageway the waiting men had slumped to the floor, their backs resting on the bulkhead. The man with the black eye looked the worst: the eye was swollen shut so that even his eyelashes weren't visible and the bruising around it had darkened. I knelt next to him and held up two fingers in front of his face. 'How many fingers do you see?' I asked. The man squinted with his good eye.

104

'I can't really tell – they're all blurry.'

'You're next.' I handed him the ice pack, which he accepted gratefully, gingerly applying it to his eye.

Another seaman had a deep cut on his thigh which he was holding together with the fingers of one hand and a tightly wound scarf.

'You're third,' I said.

'It's not that bad,' he answered. 'It's not bleeding much now.'

'You're going to need stitches,' I said. 'You can't keep holding that wound together.'

Back in the first-aid room, I found Olive spreading sulfadiazine ointment on the oiler's wound with a tongue depressor.

'But I can't go to my bunk,' he was saying to Olive. 'I'm on watch.'

Olive began to bandage the wound. 'This is a severe burn. When the morphine wears off, it will be very painful again. You'll need another shot in six hours; meet me back here and I'll take care of it. As for working, you must avoid infection. That means no dirt and oil. Get clean and stay that way, for several days. If you get any grief from the chief engineer, just tell me and I'll talk to him.' My money was on Olive's instructions being followed to the letter.

After the wiper left, the man with the black eye slid on to the gurney which served as an examination table. Olive felt around his eye while he moaned. Then she pried his eyelid open to check his eye.

'That's as bad a shiner as I've ever seen,' she said. 'I think you may have an orbital fracture.'

'What's that?' Isted asked.

'The bone around his eye socket is cracked,' she said. 'But the eye looks OK.'

'How can you tell?' he asked.

'Here – feel it,' she said, guiding Isted's fingers. 'Feel the bone give?'

The seaman yelped.

'Yeah, I feel it.'

'Am I going to go blind in that eye?' the seaman asked, frightened.

'Not if you do as I say. You need to rest for several days in case you have a concussion. Louise, can you walk him back to his bunk?'

'Sure,' I said.

'Who else is waiting in the hall?' she asked me.

'A seaman who needs stitches and a few bumps and bruises.'

'Do you know how to stitch up a cut?' she asked Isted.

'I've practiced on pigs' feet, but I've not done a person yet.'

'Now's your chance,' she said.

As I guided the wiper out into the hall, I sent the seaman who needed stitches inside.

'That woman is practically a doctor,' the man with the shiner said to the seaman as I guided him past.

I figured that ten years of nursing, much of it during wartime, could make a nurse practically a doctor. I was glad she was on our ship. We might need her again before we reached Liverpool.

After lunch – another cold meal – we went up on deck. Being confined below, even in the wardroom, after the frightening twenty-four hours we'd spent in our bunks during the gale, was too much. We wanted to be out in the fresh air. And fresh and crisp it was – twelve degrees above zero! We split off in the usual groups. The Smit family watched a signalman work on the bow. His careful arm signals, moving in set patterns, communicated with the ships in our convoy without using the radio, which might alert submarines. A stack of flags, all with different patterns, were piled in a box at his feet. The signalman wore a Navy uniform, which meant that he was part of the Navy Armed Guard under Tom's command. Another signalman worked at the stern. At lunch, Tom had told us one was 'talking' to the commodore ship and another broadcasting our coordinates to the visible ships in the convoy. Those in turn would signal to the ships they could see and so on. Tom said twenty ships were out of formation. It could take a couple of days to collect the convoy together again. He didn't say so, but I knew we'd be vulnerable to attack while we waited.

Gil and Ronan took up their usual spot at the ship's rail, watching the launch from the commodore ship heading our way.

For once, Blanche joined Olive and me. We walked the length of the ship and back, enjoying the exercise. We found the engineer's mate driving the last rivet into the repair tear in the deck. The tear was completely covered with sheet metal, secured around the edges by what looked like enough ties, bolts and rivets to hold the entire ship together.

'Think it's going to hold?' Blanche asked.

'I do,' he said. 'There's been no further tearing. And a dozen seamen have rappelled down the hull of the ship to inspect the hull. It's intact.'

The launch arrived and was met by our master, Chief Popeye and Tom. The knowledge of military uniforms I'd acquired in DC wasn't much help in identifying the contingent from the *Evans*, since they were all dressed in arctic foul-weather gear. I would guess that the officer who saluted and then shook hands with the master was the executive officer, as the commanding officer wouldn't leave the ship. He was accompanied by two others with insignia on their caps that I didn't recognize. After saluting and shaking hands, the group climbed to the bridge deck, where I could see them huddled together over the navigation map.

'I wonder what's going on?' Olive asked.

'They're figuring out how to get the convoy together and on course again,' Blanche said. 'They can't use the radio.'

Every cargo ship on its own at sea was in terrible danger.

After a few more minutes of wandering around the deck, the freezing weather defeated us and we turned and headed back amidships. Fewer seamen were now occupied with deck chores. Most of the mess caused by the storm had been cleaned up. I intended to spend the afternoon in my bunk by myself, reading or napping – I didn't care much which one. When we approached the superstructure, I noticed the group on the bridge still huddled together, talking. The officers

108

wouldn't rest until all the convoy ships were in formation again, with the defensive warships guarding their perimeter. No naps for them.

Blanche was gazing out across the deck. Olive and I followed her gaze and saw Tom calibrating the sight on one of the anti-aircraft guns. He saw us and waved. Blanche smiled, but she turned away, as if she didn't want us to notice, tripping over one of the many coils of rope that littered the deck. She might have fallen hard on a nearby metal stanchion except a seaman passing by caught her. Oddly, it seemed to me that her savior tried to turn and walk away quickly. But Blanche grasped him by his arm – to thank him, I assumed.

Instead, she screamed. And screamed again. The seaman, who was the red-headed man who'd joined the crew late while the passengers boarded back at the Navy Yard in DC, backed away. But Blanche kept her hold on him.

'Why are you here?' she shouted. 'Why? Are you following me?'

'Mrs Bryant,' the seaman began in a British accent, 'I didn't mean to shock you. Really I didn't!'

Blanche turned to us while still hanging on to the seaman. 'It's Nigel!' she shouted.

'Who?' I answered, puzzled.

'Nigel Ramsey, my late husband's orderly. He's not a seaman! Why is he on this ship? He must be spying on me!'

'Ma'am,' Nigel said, 'I had no other . . .'

'Shut up!' Blanche shouted. 'You always thought I killed Eddie! Did his parents hire you to spy on me?'

By this time a clutch of gawkers had gathered, enough that Tom had to push them aside to reach us. Olive and I had peeled Blanche's hands off Nigel, trying to calm her down. Nigel rubbed his arm where she'd gripped him.

'Blanche,' Olive said, 'we'll get to the bottom of this. Let's go down to my cabin and I'll give you something for your nerves.'

'Don't try to placate me,' Blanche said. 'I want to know what's going on!'

'So do I,' the master's voice boomed. He and Popeye stood at my shoulder.

'Mrs Bryant,' the master said, controlling his voice with difficulty, 'I'm trying to keep us from being shot out of the water. I don't have time for your personal problems. You,' he said, pointing at her and then at Nigel, 'you get to my cabin and wait there for me. Mrs Pearlie, I'd like you to join us. Ensign Banks, I have no authority to command you to do anything, but I want you there, too. Understand?'

'Yes, sir, I do.'

The master's cabin wasn't a lot larger than my berth. He had his own tiny lavatory and a small desk in addition to the standard bunk, but the floor space was still tight. None of us dared to sit on his bunk or desk chair, so we leaned against the bulkheads and waited. The master leaned against the cabin door with his arms crossed as if preventing us from escaping. A vein in his forehead pulsated. He was angry, and most of his anger was directed at Blanche.

'What in the name of bloody hell do you think

110

you are doing, screaming and squabbling on deck like that! You must be a moron not to understand the danger we're in. We're missing seventeen ships from this convoy, and we have to give them some time to find us, if they haven't been blown out of the water already. And we've been ordered to tow a corvette with engine damage while it's being repaired. So the entire convoy – or what's left of it – will travel at three knots for two days. After that, the rest of the convoy will proceed at full speed ahead of us, whether we can join them or not. Right now, a rowboat could keep up with us! All hands have been on watch for twenty-four hours! And I have to leave the bridge to deal with this! If I had known that you'd booked on my ship again, I would have forbidden it. You caused enough trouble on our last voyage.'

Blanche responded quietly. '*I* didn't cause you any trouble, Master; my late husband did. He's the one who rolled himself off the ship. You might recollect that the police, whom you felt had to be notified when we reached port, found no reason to suspect me of anything.'

The master pressed his fingers against his forehead before answering. 'All right, forget it. So what was your public screaming fit about?'

Blanche pointed at Nigel. 'This man. You might recognize him. He's masquerading as a merchant seaman. He's Nigel Ramsey, my late husband's orderly. I think he must be spying on me, maybe for my husband's family. They think I murdered him – thanks in part to you.'

The master jerked forward and grabbed Nigel's watch cap off his head, revealing his full head of red hair. 'By God, it *is* you! What the hell are you doing here? Show me your seaman's card.'

Nigel pulled his identification card out of his shirt pocket and handed it over to the master, who read the name on it. 'Alan Starkey,' he said. 'Where did you get this? Did you steal it?'

'No, sir,' he said. 'I found it.'

'Sure you did. I should throw you in the brig! Is Mrs Bryant correct? Are you spying on her?'

Nigel glanced at Blanche before he spoke to the master. 'Master, I swear to you I had no idea that Mrs Bryant would be on this ship. I just wanted to get back to England. When Mr Bryant's family fired me, they didn't pay me! I couldn't find a job because I didn't have a reference from them. I slept in churches and ate at soup kitchens! When I found the seaman's card, I got the idea to work my way back to England. It was just luck I wound up on the *Amelia Earhart*.'

The master stared at Nigel, but he didn't blink. 'All right,' he said. 'We need every man we have, and you seem to have done acceptable work. You get back to your station and don't tell a soul about this conversation or I'll keelhaul you. Got it?'

'Yes, sir,' Nigel said. He was out of the door in two seconds flat.

'But, Master—' Blanche began.

He raised his hand to stop her. 'It's not against maritime law to send a woman to the brig,' he said. 'I don't want to hear a word from you, or about you, or about your late husband, again. Understand?'

Blanche was white with fury, but she had the

112

sense to know the conversation was over. 'Yes,' she said.

'Mrs Pearlie, you are here because I want you to know what's going on, so that you can talk sense into this woman when it's required. Understand?'

I nodded. I was appalled to be given the task of supervising Blanche, but I could see it was unavoidable.

The master turned on Tom next. 'Ensign Bates,' he said, 'you do realize there are strict regulations against fraternizing with the casual passengers aboard, do you not?'

Tom opened his mouth, surprised. 'Sir, I don't know what you mean.'

'This ship is rife with rumors that you and Mrs Bryant are romancing each other while we are trying to get across miles of frozen ocean to the UK without getting our asses blown off by a torpedo finding its way to our hold full of munitions.'

'That's just ship gossip. I swear Mrs Bryant and I are only friends,' Tom said.

'I don't give a damn what you swear,' he said. 'You focus on your job or I'll see that you lose your commission.'

'Yes, sir.'

'Get out of my sight, all of you.'

I got as far out of everyone's sight as I could. I needed to be alone to think, and I didn't want to be squashed in my tiny berth. Dressed in three layers of clothing, my peacoat and watch hat, I wandered the deck looking for a spot to

113

be alone and think. I found myself standing next to the train locomotive traveling to Europe on the deck of the *Amelia Earhart*. It was so out of place at sea, even more so than the other vehicles, that it brought a smile to my face. So I climbed into it and sat right down at the controls. I'd ridden on plenty of trains, but never in the engine. The levers, dials and buttons meant nothing to me, but in that space I had the quiet I needed to think.

Maybe I'd worked for a spy organization long enough now that every odd incident looked like a conspiracy, but Eddie Bryant's death niggled at me, even though suicide was an obvious explanation. The man was crippled for life, his marriage was unhappy and, according to everyone who knew him, he had a vile disposition. He was mean to his wife, his orderly and the passengers who tried to be friendly with him.

I remembered how brave Phoebe's son, Milt, had been when he came home after he lost his left arm. Yes, he drank too much for a time, yes, he was short-tempered occasionally, yes, he spent hours on his bed with his cigarettes and records some days, but his basic attitude was to move on with his life, even if he didn't know how. He insisted on working, even though the only job he could find at first was as an elevator operator. He made himself go out with old friends despite his self-consciousness. He practiced doing everyday tasks with one arm. It seemed that Eddie Bryant had not possessed any such admirable qualities.

So perhaps Bryant had killed himself. But I

wondered. Why did Blanche spend no time with him, and why did he dislike her so much? I thought that must be due to problems in the marriage before his injury. Were she and Tom having an affair, either on the way from England to the States or on this voyage? Or both? It seemed likely; she was absent from her berth so much that if she wasn't with him, what was she doing? Of course, they would both deny it. I hated to think that Tom might be involved in Eddie Bryant's death, but reason required me to accept that possibility. Where was Tom when Eddie was left alone on deck? If he wasn't on watch, he could have been with Blanche. Blanche said she'd been elsewhere on deck, but had anyone seen her? Why did Nigel leave Eddie alone at the rail of the ship for the time it took him to fetch a cigarette lighter from their stateroom? Just about everyone on board ship smoked; Nigel could have bummed a match from a passing seaman. And could it be a coincidence that Nigel signed on to the *Amelia Earhart* for its return trip to England? If it wasn't a coincidence, what was his reason? Was he spying on Blanche on behalf of the Bryant family? And Tom, too? My head was aching with the effort of sorting it all out. In the end I had nothing. Just a series of events that I couldn't link together in any way that indicated that Eddie Bryant's death was anything other than suicide.

I was thinking of going back to my berth when I heard Grace singing. That woman had a lovely voice. The mellow sound of 'Take the A Train' floated up to me, reminding me of records and the radio, which I missed so much. I poked my head out of the engine window. 'Hi, Grace,' I called out. 'I'm up here!'

I startled her. She jerked back and looked up at me, her hand on her heart. 'Oh, my goodness, Mrs Pearlie! You scared me!'

'Come on up and join me,' I said. 'The view is great.'

Grace looked around, checking to see if anyone saw her. Then she climbed the few steps to the locomotive cab to join me. 'What on earth possessed you to come up here?' she asked, as she sat next to me in the cab.

'I couldn't bear the thought of my little berth or of making small talk in the wardroom, and it's cold on deck. Up here, the windows in the cab keep out the wind.'

'There aren't many places to go on this ship to get away,' she said. 'I'm the only colored woman on board this trip, so I have my own berth, but it's right next to the galley. It's so noisy! And since the cooks have to fix food for all the watches, it's noisy twenty-four hours a day!'

From our perch we watched the crew get a cable on the crippled corvette. A dinghy with several seamen, hunched into their collars with their sou'westers pulled low over their faces, carried the line, which uncoiled from a winch on our deck, to the corvette. Its crewmembers hauled the line aboard and fastened it to a stanchion.

'I hope it doesn't take long for the corvette's engines to be repaired. We're sitting ducks out here,' I said.

'I heard in the mess that it should only take a

116

couple of days. Then the convoy will have to return to its regular speed and course.'

'What if all the scattered ships haven't found us yet?'

She shrugged. 'We'll keep signaling and sounding our foghorns. But if they don't link up, they're on their own.'

We weren't even a third of the way to our destination yet. That was a long way for a single ship without an armed escort to travel over this cold and deadly ocean.

Grace and I both fell silent, thinking, I assumed, of the same thing: the fate of the ships that didn't make it back to the convoy. Then I heard Grace sniffling, and when I looked at her, I saw tears running down her face.

'Sweetie,' I said, 'what's wrong?'

'Everything,' she said, and leaned her head on my shoulder, sobbing.

I didn't know what to do except to comfort her as best I could. I put an arm around her shoulder, lent her my handkerchief and patted her hand.

'Can I help?' I said. 'What's wrong?'

'No,' she said. 'I can't say anything. I don't dare. If it got out!'

'You can tell me anything,' I said. 'I'm good at keeping secrets.'

'Really?'

'Yes, really.'

'You won't tell?'

'Of course not.'

'It's Nigel!' she said, and then burst into tears again.

Nigel? The only Nigel I knew was Eddie

117

Bryant's orderly, who'd posed as a seaman to get a ride back to England. Could he be the person Grace was crying over?

'Nigel and me . . . well, he's my sweetheart. OK! You're shocked, I know,' Grace said.

Not shocked so much as concerned. Segregation of the colored race from the rest of society was the law in the United States. And a romantic relationship between a man and woman of different races would be just plain dangerous to any couple tempted to date or marry. I had been raised to believe that miscegenation was wrong, but I had lived in DC for two years, where I had met every sort of person from banished kings to homosexuals. My brain was my own and I'd concluded that segregation and prejudice were wrong. I admired Eleanor Roosevelt's fight against it. So I was more worried for Grace than I was shocked.

Of course, Britain wasn't segregated. Grace and Nigel could court there.

'You see,' Grace said, 'we got to be friends on the voyage from England to the States. Nigel was Mr Bryant's orderly, you know. And Nigel was always kind to him. I don't know how he did it day after day. Anyway, when I was off watch, I sometimes sat with Mr Bryant so Nigel could take a break.'

A loud huzzah sounded from the ship, as the cable between the damaged corvette and the Amelia Earhart held. I felt the ship shudder as the cable went taut.

'Everyone has said Mr Bryant was unpleasant,' I said.

118

'Once when I came to sit with him, I went into the room just as he threw an ashtray at Mr Gil. Later Mr Gil told me he only offered to play cards with him. And Nigel said that Mr Bryant kept saying that he wasn't responsible for the plane crash, that there was something wrong with the plane. He said he would sue the people responsible for crippling him when he got home.

'Who was he going to sue? Hitler? Anyway, once Mr Bryant was settled in bed with his book at night, Nigel would come on deck and we'd find a spot to sit and talk. We couldn't go to the mess hall for fear people would stare at us. We liked each other. Is that such a crime?'

'No, it's not,' I said.

'After Mr Bryant died, Nigel was in an awful spot. He had no place to stay and no job. He just wanted to get back to England, but he didn't have the money for a ticket. My auntie let him sleep on the sofa. I knew I would be headed back to England in a few weeks and we wanted to be together.'

'Nigel said he found the ID card,' I said.

'No. I bought it from an old seaman who had lost his leg,' Grace said. 'I knew that cargo ships were always short-handed, so Nigel just showed up at the *Amelia Earhart* and got a spot on the departure day. We were lucky.'

'What are you and Nigel going to do when we get to Liverpool?'

I'd asked the wrong question. Grace started to cry again.

'Sweetie, don't; it'll be OK,' I said.

By now my handkerchief was too damp to do

119

her much good, so Grace wiped her face with her scarf. 'Nigel said that the master almost put him in the brig! What if he has him arrested when we get to Liverpool?'

'I heard that conversation,' I said. 'The master was much angrier at Blanche than he was with Nigel. He said Nigel was a good worker and he needed him to stay on duty. I bet once we get to Liverpool we can talk the master into letting Nigel off the hook. He should stay out of the master's way until then. And the two of you need to be careful, too.' It might be legal in England for Nigel and Grace to court, but most of the people on board were Americans. And England wasn't short of racial prejudice either, despite its laws.

'I know,' she said. 'We are careful. Even if we do make it to Liverpool without getting drowned and Nigel doesn't get arrested, I'll only have a couple of weeks off before I get a new assignment. And I can't resign from the merchant marine during wartime.'

I wanted to tell her that if Nigel loved her, he'd wait for her, but it seemed like such a platitude that I didn't say anything. It was wartime. Nothing was guaranteed.

On the third morning after the gale, the corvette's engine fired up and its crew cast off our cable line. A huzzah went up from our seamen on deck as it was reeled in. The *Evans* signaled us to increase our speed to nine knots and remain on course.

Three of the ships in our convoy never found

us. All three were cargo ships. Three cargo ships without a defensive escort. If they weren't lost for good, we just had to pray they could find their own way to Liverpool. It was impossible to use the radio to try to locate them; it would broadcast our own position to the enemy. The only use of the radio that was allowed was reception, short bursts of weather forecasts or enemy sightings. So if a German submarine surfaced in our midst, we could broadcast that! The three Sparks spent most of their time stretched out on a cot in the radio room reading comic books.

We didn't have any idea what was happening in the rest of the world. I thought I would miss the world news, but I didn't. It was a relief not to hear of the terrible things going on in the war, day in and day out. I did miss music, though. Especially the Grand Ole Opry. My fellow boarders used to tease me about my love of 'hill-billy' music. It would be a long time before I heard 'Wildwood Flower' or 'Great Speckled Bird' again. I suspected that the Carter Family and Roy Acuff weren't big in England.

I'd read both of the books I'd brought with me and Olive's, too. In desperation, I rummaged through the dog-eared paperbacks in the ship's library, which is how I found myself wrapped in blankets in my bunk deep in Zane Grey's *Riders of the Purple Sage*. The heroine was a Utah rancher named Jane Withersteen whose livelihood was threatened by a marriage she did not want. Until a lone cowboy named Lassiter came to town. I could not put it down.

I heard light footsteps running down the

gangway and then a small hand knocking at my door. I knew it was Corrie Smit.

'Come in, Corrie,' I said.

Corrie burst into my berth, her hair flying behind her and her scarf trailing the floor.

'Mrs Pearlie, Miss Olive says you have to come out on deck! You won't believe it!'

'Oh, Corrie, not now,' I said. 'I'm reading such a good book. And it's freezing outside.'

'You have to come! There's an iceberg!'

It was an iceberg, all right. Of course, I had never seen one before. Corrie and Alida and I crowded together on the ship's rail to gawk. It was huge, towering over us. When the sun poked through the clouds, it sparkled like diamonds. One side was steep and vertical – from sheering cleanly off its mother ice field, I assumed. The other side was ragged and battered, as if waves had been beating on it forever. Two spires, as tall as church steeples, rose from the main ice mass. Seabirds, mostly gulls and terns, careened around it, squawking. They'd land on it in groups, socialize, eat a little something, groom themselves, then take off again with beating wings.

I couldn't get over how enormous it was. 'It's like a floating mountain,' I said to the girls.

'Iceberg comes from a Dutch word,' Alida said. '*Ijsberg*. It means ice mountain.'

Tom joined us at the rail. 'Are we far enough away from it?' I asked him. 'Isn't an iceberg much larger under the surface of the water?' I was thinking of the *Titanic*, of course.

'We're taking constant soundings,' he said.

'We're at a safe distance. But darn, it's big! The old-timers on the crew are saying it's the biggest iceberg they've ever seen. I wish I could stay and admire it, but I've got to go talk to Sparks. The master wants us to broadcast the berg's coordinates to the convoy.' So this giant white mountain was dangerous enough to break radio silence.

Ronan took Tom's place at the rail. He was wrapped in his tweed coat, wearing a flat cap with a scarf tied over it and his chin. He smelled of pipe tobacco.

'I just talked to Chief Pitts,' Ronan said. 'He measured it somehow from the bridge deck. He says it's over two hundred and ten feet tall at the tip of the highest spire.'

'That's more than twenty stories!' Taller than most of the buildings in DC.

News of the magnitude of our iceberg spread to the crew members who weren't on watch, and soon the decks were packed with seaman staring up at the berg with hands shading their eyes. The boat deck, which was a level above the main deck, was crowded too. I noticed Nigel there, leaning over the rail, in a group with his British buddies. The Smits were with me and Ronan at the main deck rail, while Olive stood on a cable spool behind us so she could see over our heads. The master was on the bridge deck with binoculars to his eyes.

I wasn't surprised not to see Gil or Blanche. Gil was too worldly to be interested in something as mundane as an iceberg. Blanche was avoiding people even more than usual. After her public hissy fit on deck when she'd recognized Nigel, she'd even taken to eating her meals in her cabin.

Our ship and the iceberg drifted apart quickly. The berg was headed south to melt, while we were steaming east to England. The sun vanished behind another bank of gray cloud and the wind whipped up again. The crowd on deck wandered back to their berths or their watch duties. Tom never rejoined us; something must have distracted him.

Mrs Smit touched my arm. 'Grace should have the coffee down below by now,' she said. 'We're going inside. Want to join us?'

'I'll be right behind you,' I said. 'I'm going to tell Olive where I'm headed.'

'I'll come when I've finished my pipe,' Ronan said.

Olive decided she was ready for a cup of coffee too, so we went inside the door to the head of the stairway to our berths. That was when we heard the screaming. Olive, with her nurse's training, reacted first, running for the head of the staircase. I was right behind her. We both scrambled down and found the Smit women gathered around someone lying at the bottom. They'd stopped screaming, but Alida and Corrie were sobbing.

Grace lay splayed at the foot of the stairs. Her eyes were open wide, staring at the ceiling. Olive knelt next to her and felt for her pulse, then shook her head. Grace was dead.

Nine

'What a bloody shame,' the master said. 'Damn it! I'll have to telegraph her parents when we get to port.'

'She was a good girl,' the chief steward said. 'A good worker. Everyone liked her.'

Olive and I had stayed with Grace's body while Mrs Smit took her daughters back to their berth. Mr Smit had rushed up the steps and straight to the bridge to tell the master what had happened. The master sent a seaman to notify Chief Pearce, who was Grace's boss. When Chief Pearce arrived, he knelt next to Grace and gently closed her staring eyes. 'I'll get a blanket to cover her,' he said, straightening up and going down the passageway toward the steward's closet.

My OSS training kicked in and I took in the entire scene of Grace's death before it was disturbed. I could hardly look at her, but I forced myself. It seemed clear that she'd fallen down the stairs and died from severe head injuries. The tray she'd been carrying lay in our passageway; its contents – coffee pot, tea, mugs, sugar and milk – had spilled all over the floor. Broken cookies were scattered about. Oatmeal raisin.

The chief steward returned with a blanket. He and Olive wrapped it neatly around Grace's body. 'I just don't understand,' the chief steward said, as he carefully lifted Grace's head to enclose it

125

in the blanket. I could see a large dark bruise on the back of her head from where I stood. Maybe she had ruptured a blood vessel. 'Grace was so agile; she went up and down ladders, through gangways during storms, like a squirrel in his favorite tree. Why did she fall in calm weather down the safest stair on the ship?' he said.

The master, who'd been standing with his arms crossed for minutes now, must have been thinking along the same lines, because he said, 'I wonder if something distracted her? So that she missed a step and fell?'

'We'll never know,' the chief steward said. 'There were no witnesses. The Smits found her when they came inside to get their coffee.'

'Everyone was on deck, looking at the iceberg,' I said.

'I'll lay her out in the first-aid room,' the chief steward said. 'The door locks.'

'I'll help,' Olive said.

'We'll bury her at sea tomorrow afternoon,' the master said. The chief steward lifted Grace's torso and Olive took her legs. They carried her up the stairway, cautiously.

'Someone needs to clean this up,' I said, noticing the messy floor. The spilled coffee and litter from Grace's tray covered the passageway.

'The chief will send a messman down to clean,' the master said.

'Will there be an inquiry?' I asked.

The master shrugged. 'No. It's not necessary. My report will read that Grace died when she fell down the stairs. It was an accident. There's nothing else to say.'

126

Now that Grace's body had been moved, I began to feel the physical impact of her death. I felt woozy and grabbed the stair handrail. The master put a hand on one of my shoulders and squeezed it. 'You look quite pale, Mrs Pearlie,' he said. 'Why don't you rest in your berth for a while? The messman will have all this cleaned up very soon.'

'There's Nigel,' I said.

'Who?'

'Nigel, the British boy, Mr Bryant's orderly, who sneaked on board the ship pretending to be a seaman,' I said. 'He and Grace were sweethearts.'

'Swell,' he said. 'Another complication. I'll call him to the bridge. Maybe I'll be able to tell him before he hears the news.' He ran his hand under his cap through graying hair. 'I've never been good at delivering bad news. I hate it.'

By the time I reached the door to my berth, I could feel the tears coming, but I managed to get inside before breaking down. I don't know how long I lay curled up on my bunk, crying. Poor Grace. What a waste of a life. She'd had so many hopes and plans. Stupid, stupid war. I thought of all the families, worldwide, Axis and Allied, who'd lost loved ones. It was a wonder the earth hadn't collapsed under the weight of their grief.

It was dark outside when someone knocked on my door. I recognized Olive's knock and thought of not answering but didn't want to worry her. 'Come on in,' I said.

Olive sat down on my bunk next to me and took my hands. 'How are you?' she asked.

127

'Awful. I don't feel well.'

'You're in shock. Come with me; you need food and drink to recover from it.'

'The last thing I want to do is go to dinner.'

'I'll bring you a sandwich and some milk, OK?'

'I'd appreciate that. Does everyone know about Grace?'

'Yes. Ronan and Gil ran into the chief steward and me carrying Grace's body to the first-aid room. Of course, they were horrified. Blanche turned up just as the messman was cleaning the passageway. She was so upset; I was surprised to see her showing that much feeling, I didn't think she had it in her.'

'Where had she been?'

'Said she'd been on the boat deck looking at the iceberg with everyone else.'

I didn't see her there, but then the deck was jam-packed, everyone wearing dark coats and hats. I could have missed her easily.

Olive left me to go to dinner.

I exchanged grief for worry. I didn't agree with the master that there was no need to conduct an inquiry into Grace's death. I didn't think the circumstances of her accident were as simple as he did. In fact, it wasn't reasonable to me that Grace would have fallen in the first place. She'd lectured all of us on how to go up and down our staircase and the ladders on the ship. I'd seen her many times coming down, her left hand gripping the rail, her right holding her tray or a stack of linens up against her hip, ready to drop if the ship lurched and she needed to hang on to the rail with both hands. And the ship hadn't been

128

lurching; the sea had been calm. And if she had fallen, how did the tray and its contents wind up in the passageway below? She would have had to fling it over the rail. If she'd fallen down and dropped it, as the master speculated, the tray and its contents would have scattered on the stairs.

I pulled my musette bag out of the drawer under my bed and drew out a small notebook and a pencil. I was not much of an artist, but for this purpose stick figures would suffice.

So I drew the scene as I remembered it. Short parallel horizontal lines down the left side of the page were the stairs, as though a witness was looking at the scene from its foot. A long vertical line edging the stairs on the right represented the stair rail. Grace's body lay face up at the foot of the staircase. The tray and its contents were scattered in the passageway. I stuck the pencil in my mouth while I contemplated my rudimentary drawing.

What I saw didn't jibe with the master's and the chief steward's conclusion that Grace had fallen down the stairs to her death. It seemed more likely to me that she had reached the bottom of the stairs and turned to go down the passageway when she was struck from behind by someone. Hard enough to fracture her skull. She'd dropped to the floor, dead, and her tray and its contents spilled all over the passageway floor. Then her killer positioned her body at the bottom of the stairs so that it looked as though she had fallen from above. And fled. He, or she, would have had time, both to do the deed and to escape, because everyone was on deck admiring the iceberg. No matter how I went over my drawing, this scenario seemed the most feasible. I was determined to discuss this with the master. After all, I was not without experience. I was practically a spy.

I slipped outside my berth into the passageway. A messman had cleaned after Grace's body had been moved, but still I examined the stairs and the passageway for any marks that might indicate how Grace had fallen. I'd brought my flashlight with me. I went up the stairs and worked my way down them. Pausing at the brass finial on top of the newel post, I wondered if she could have smacked into it in a fall. But I couldn't picture how she might have hit the back of her head. There were no marks on the knob either.

The passageway was spotless, mopped by the messman. From where Grace's tray had landed, I looked up at the staircase. The gaps between the posts supporting the handrail were too narrow for the tray to pass through as Grace fell. If she'd fallen, I didn't see how the tray could have found its way over the handrail. It should have fallen down the stairs with her.

If, as I speculated, someone had hit Grace on the back of the head as she turned from the staircase to go down the passageway, what might he or she have hit her with? Just about anything, I thought. The ship was full of hard metal gear that could have been used, then wiped and replaced. Everything from a fire ax to a wrench.

The only thing I noticed that might prove useful was that the lavatory was at the end of the section of the passageway that would have been behind Grace. Someone could have heard her coming, hidden in it and then attacked her when she turned her back. Of course, it would need to be a person who wasn't on deck admiring the iceberg.

'Oh, Louise,' Olive said. 'I'm sure you're wrong.'

Olive had brought me a ham sandwich and a glass of milk. She studied my primitive drawing while I ate the sandwich.

'Why?' I said.

'Because it makes no sense. Who would want to murder Grace? I was fond of her too, but she was just the colored stewardess. I'm sure she fell. Maybe not exactly the way the master speculated, but she wasn't killed by anybody.'

I tapped the paper she held in her hand. 'Is this a decent representation of what the scene looked like?'

'Yes, it is.'

'Then explain to me how the tray, coffeepot and food got on to the passageway floor. Grace would have dropped it on the steps. She would be grabbing at the rail with both hands to try to stop her fall.'

'I don't know, Louise, I wasn't there, but I'm sure you're wrong. No one saw what happened, but there has to be an explanation for her fall that doesn't involve murder. That's a loony idea. Why would anyone want to kill Grace?'

That question again. I had no answer.

I was about to argue when someone knocked on the door. It was the chief steward.

'Come in,' I said. 'Please.'

131

The chief steward stood, with his cap in hand, in the entrance of the door. 'I'm glad you're both here,' he said. 'I have a favor to ask.'

'Sure,' I said.

'We want everything to be done proper for Grace. The funeral is tomorrow afternoon, and, well, we want her to be . . . you know . . .'

'You want us to prepare her body and dress her?' Olive asked. My ham sandwich turned somersaults in my stomach. I couldn't, I just couldn't.

'Yes, ma'am, it wouldn't be right for, you know, a man to do it. And I thought you being a nurse, and Mrs Pearlie being her friend, you might be willing.'

'Of course we are,' I said.

The chief steward was intensely relieved. 'After breakfast tomorrow I'll unlock her berth for you,' he said, 'So you can choose her clothes and such. And then I'll take you to the first-aid room. It's private there.'

After he left, Olive took my hands again. 'I can do this by myself,' Olive said. 'I've prepared corpses for burial before.'

'No,' I said, 'I want to help. I can do it.' I would do this final thing for Grace. Besides, this would give me – *us*, because Olive was going to help me even if she didn't know it yet – the chance to examine Grace's body. Maybe we could find more physical evidence as to how she died.

It was a one-egg day. With waffles. Maybe the cooks were trying to cheer us up. Except that every person in the mess hall and wardroom was profoundly conscious that Grace would never again enjoy a fried egg with bacon and waffles. It reminded me that there were small pleasures in life that made it worth living, even in the midst of a world war.

As I carried my tray through the mess hall to the wardroom, I saw Nigel valiantly trying to eat something, encouraged by a couple of his fellow seamen from England. He looked stricken. Occasionally, someone would come up to him, squeeze him on the shoulder and say a few words before passing by. Poor man.

I put down my tray at the table with the Smits, Olive and Blanche. Every eye was red-rimmed from crying. We ate in silence; even Alida had nothing to say. Gil, who'd been sitting with Ronan and Tom nearby, brought the coffee pot to our table.

'Coffee?' he said. The Smits drank tea, but the rest of us were happy for him to refill our cups.

I had slept little. I had spent the night fighting myself, one minute sure that Grace's death had not been an accident, the other that she fell in some manner that scattered her tray in the passageway and I just didn't understand how. I sipped my fresh cup of coffee and told myself I'd simply concentrate on getting myself through this day.

Gil pulled up a chair. He awkwardly patted my hand. 'How are you all doing?' he asked. None of us said anything, although Corrie sniffled. After a minute he cleared his throat. 'Does anyone know if there will be an inquiry into Grace's death?'

133

'I don't think so,' Olive said. 'The master said there wasn't any time for that, since the fall was an accident. He's going to write an incident report.'

'The proper authorities must be notified,' Smit said. 'And the child's poor parents.'

'Since no one saw what happened, I suppose that makes sense,' Gil said. 'We were all on deck, gawking at the iceberg, except for the crew on watch.'

As casually as I could, I said, 'Where were you, Gil? I didn't see you.'

He didn't hesitate. 'Ronan and I were on the boat deck.'

'Ronan was at the rail with us.'

'He left the deck to get closer to the berg. I've seen icebergs before. After you and Olive left, I joined him and smoked a cigarette until he finished his pipe, and we went below.' Gil didn't mention running into the chief steward and Olive carrying Grace, I supposed to spare the feelings of the Smit girls. I hadn't seen Gil at the rail of the boat deck myself, but it had been so crowded I could have missed him.

The chief steward stood up from his table and caught our eye. Olive and I joined him as he left the wardroom.

Chief Pearce unlocked a small metal door not far from the galley and ushered us into Grace's berth. He stood in the doorway, since there wasn't room for all of us to stand inside. There was barely room for Olive and me. Two bunks took up almost all the space in the tiny berth, which must have been designed for a couple of messmen

134

to share. Since Grace was a woman, she had had the space to herself.

'OK,' Chief Pearce said. 'I'll meet you at the first-aid room in half an hour? Will that give you enough time to take care of her things?'

'Sure,' I said. 'We'll see you then.'

Grace had kept her duffle bag on the top bunk secured to a hand grip. There was no place else to put it. Her pocket book was in the drawer under the bottom bunk with her clothes and other items. A toiletry bag, hairbrush, rollers and a makeup kit. Two books, both by Zora Neal Hurston. She had the usual underclothes, trousers, sweaters and work clothes. Two nightgowns. Her coat. And the matching Dutch bonnet and scarf she was wearing when I first met her. At the very bottom of her drawer we were surprised to find a woman's merchant mariner uniform. Officially, the merchant marine was under the command of the US Navy during the war, and mariners did have uniforms. So far, I hadn't seen anyone wear one, even the officers. It just wasn't part of their tradition. Many of the crew didn't bother to purchase one.

I held the uniform up for Olive to see. 'Do you think we should dress her in this?' I asked.

'Absolutely,' she said.

I wrapped the uniform, a pair of black pumps and the appropriate undergarments in a bundle while Olive packed Grace's suitcase with the rest of her things. A square of paper fell out of one of the paperbacks and Olive picked it up. 'Oh, God,' she said.

'What is it?'

Olive handed the paper to me. It was a photograph of Grace and Nigel taken at a photo booth somewhere. Two happy young people mugging at the camera. I tucked it into my sweater pocket. 'I'll give it to Nigel,' I said.

The chief steward was waiting for us outside the first-aid room. He unlocked the door for us. We handed over Grace's suitcase to him and he gave us a package. 'It's a shroud,' he said. 'Once you've dressed the body, zip it up in this. We'll load ballast into it later. I'll give you a key to lock up when you're done.'

We went into the first-aid room and closed the door behind us. Grace's body lay under the blanket she'd been wrapped in after her death. Olive pulled it off her. The sight wasn't awful, just desperately sad. Grace's lifeless body, with its soul departed, lay there like an abandoned doll. The bruise on the back of her neck and head had darkened since we had first seen her body.

'Well,' Olive said. 'Let's get this over with.' She began to unbutton Grace's sweater.

'Wait a minute,' I said.

'It's OK; if you don't feel well, I can do it.'

'It's not that. Before we dress her, I'd like to look at her body. Closely.'

'What are you talking about?'

'There's no doctor on board to do a post-mortem. I think we should look her over for any evidence of how she died.'

'She died from a head injury. Look at that bruising – it's clear.'

'It won't take long. I think it's important.'

Olive rolled her eyes. 'All right, why not.' We undressed her quickly. What we saw was not what we expected. Her skin was clear and flawless. Not a mark on it, no scar, no birth marks. 'Roll her over and I'll look at her back,' Olive said. I did, and Olive looked. 'I don't understand,' she said. 'This young woman didn't fall down any stairs. There's not a bruise on her body.'

I was surprised. Despite my worries, I'd fully expected to find some evidence of a fall on Grace's body. Olive covered Grace up to her neck and we turned our attention to her head wound. Olive directed me to hold Grace's head up while she examined it. I turned away. When I turned back, Olive was washing her hands.

'She had a skull fracture, I can feel the depression. The injury was at the base of her neck and caused blood vessels to rupture.'

'So she could have been hit hard from behind, with a heavy object?' I said.

'Or taken a serious fall, but with no other bruising or marks on her body.'

'You said that wasn't possible.'

Olive rubbed the back of one of her shoulders. 'I don't know. I don't know what to think. Let's get her dressed.'

We bathed Grace and dressed her neatly in her uniform. Then Olive lifted her and I tucked the open shroud under her. The room went dark. I saw bright spots in front of my eyes and heard a roaring in my ears. The next time I was aware of anything, I was sitting on the floor. Olive was next to me pressing hard on the back of my neck. 'You fainted,' she said. 'Let's get you out of here.'

I let her help me to my feet and ease me into a sitting position in the hall outside. 'I'll be right back.' Olive went back inside.

I had never fainted before. I was drenched with sweat, shivering, and had a headache threatening.

Olive came back out, locking the door behind her.

'I'm sorry,' I said.

'Don't be silly. You've had enough to deal with for one day, that's all. Let's get you into your bunk. You need to rest.'

Ten

'We brought nothing into this world, and it is certain we can carry nothing out,' the master read to the crew assembled for Grace's burial. 'The Lord gave, and the Lord hath taken away; blessed be the name of the Lord.'

The entire crew of the *Amelia Earhart*, except those on watch, had assembled for Grace's burial. Usually rough and world-weary seamen stood solemnly in orderly rows, watch caps in hand, heads bowed. The master and his officers wore their merchant marine uniforms, the first time I had seen them. Tom and the rest of the Navy Armed Guard were wearing their Navy dress blues. No one seemed to feel the cold.

A bugler stepped forward from among the Navy men and lifted his instrument to his lips. The first chords of the Navy hymn, 'For Those in Peril on the Sea', sounded as Grace's body, wrapped in her shroud and draped with an American flag, was carried on a wooden plank toward the side of the ship by Nigel, the chief steward and four colored seamen. They walked steadily from amidships until they could lift the plank and rest its foot on the side rail of the ship. As the last notes of the hymn faded away, the master stepped forward.

The burial service was short; we were at war, after all. 'Unto Almighty God we commend the soul of our sister departed, Grace Bell, and we

139

commit her body to the deep; in sure and certain hope of the Resurrection unto eternal life, through our Lord Jesus Christ; at whose coming in glorious majesty to judge the world, the sea shall give up her dead; and the corruptible bodies of those who sleep in him shall be changed and made unto like his glorious body; according to the mighty working whereby he is able to subdue all things unto himself.'

The master raised his hand, and the bugler began to play 'Taps'. The pallbearers lifted the head of the wooden plank so Grace's shrouded corpse could slide gently over the rail. The chief steward gripped the flag that draped the body as it dropped into the ocean. He and Nigel folded it and handed it to the master, who would send it to Grace's family. The last notes of 'Taps' faded away.

The brief funeral service that the master had read was from the Episcopal Prayer Book. I was sure that if Grace's send-off had been in her own family's Baptist church, it would have been longer and louder. The hymns alone would have lifted off the church's roof. But I was pleased at how respectfully her service had been conducted. The crew was genuinely sorrowful; I saw plenty of sad faces in the crowd as it dispersed.

I found Nigel at the rail, staring out into the ocean. He was dry-eyed, but his face was still drawn with grief. I touched his shoulder to get his attention and he turned to me.

'The service was lovely, don't you think?' he asked. 'Very comforting.'

'Yes,' I answered, 'it was very nice.' I would

140

have felt comforted myself if I hadn't been so unsure of whether Grace's death was accidental. I'd need to make a decision soon about approaching the master. There's was no way I could allow Grace's murder – if it *was* murder – to pass without justice being done.

'The chief steward told me that you and Miss Olive . . . well, took care of Grace,' he said. 'Thank you.'

'You're welcome.' I pulled the photograph I'd found in one of Grace's books out of my pocket. 'Here,' I said, 'I found this in Grace's things.'

Nigel smiled when he took it from me. 'We took this in a photo booth at the National Zoo. We had so much fun that day.' He slipped the photo into his shirt pocket.

'What will you do now?' I asked.

'I have no idea. I'd planned my future around Grace. It would have been hard for us, even living in London, but we would have made it. Honestly, if the master threw me in the brig and left me there, I wouldn't care.'

Olive and I caught the master outside his cabin door just as he went off watch. Olive went with me reluctantly, but I needed her to testify to the condition of Grace's body.

'What now?' the master asked when he saw us waiting for him.

'We need to talk to you.'

He rolled his eyes, but he opened his cabin door and ushered us inside. We sat on the edge of his bunk while he took the desk chair.

'Out with it,' he said. 'I need to get some sleep.'

He did look tired. He was an old man doing a young man's job. And I was going to make it harder.

'I believe there's a good reason to think Grace's death wasn't an accident,' I said.

'Oh, for God's sake,' the master said. 'You're civilians. Women! What do you know?'

That got Olive's dander up. 'Master, that girl's body had not a mark on it. If she'd fallen down those stairs, she'd have been covered with bruises. I'm a nurse. I know what I'm talking about.'

'Look,' he said, 'I apologize for being rude. Maybe the girl didn't fall down the stairs. Maybe she slipped and cracked her head on something. Like a riser, or the finial on the banister.'

'Or someone hit her, hard, from behind,' I said.

The master struggled to control his temper. After a minute he spoke quietly. 'I don't know exactly what happened to Grace. There were no witnesses. But I know she wasn't murdered. She was just a colored girl, a room stewardess. Why would anyone want to kill her? When I file my report with the Maritime Commission, I'll take note of your observations. That's all I can do.'

'Master—' I began again.

'We are coming upon the most dangerous part of our voyage,' he interrupted. 'The nearer we get to England, the more German submarines and planes are waiting to attack us. I don't have time for this. Go back to your quarters and play bridge or something. Leave the running of the ship to me and my officers.'

We'd been dismissed.

* * *

142

Why would anyone kill Grace? I had no idea. So I had no motive. What about opportunity? Grace died when the usual routines of the ship were disrupted by the iceberg sighting. At the time it seemed that everyone who wasn't a crew member on watch was outside, ogling the ice mountain. Grace was on watch, preparing the tray of coffee and cookies for our hall, then carrying it downstairs, then falling and dying. Or being murdered? Who was missing from the deck or from work? I didn't see how I could figure that out. The iceberg created too much confusion on deck. If I could even locate a few people of the hundred or so on the ship who didn't have an alibi for the time of Grace's death, all they needed to say was that they were behind a piece of cargo somewhere smoking a cigarette. I was beginning to see the master's point. There was no way to prove that Grace hadn't simply fallen to her death.

Except for her unmarked body. And the scattering of her tray's contents in an unlikely place. I couldn't forget either circumstance.

Olive, Gil, Ronan and I agreed to gather for cocktails before dinner. Way before dinner. We needed a drink – or two. I insisted on inviting Blanche to join us, if only because it was the polite thing to do. I had my bottle of gin in my hand when I knocked on her door.

Blanche opened it. We both stared at each other in surprise. I was surprised to find her actually in her berth. She was surprised that someone had bothered to drop by.

'Louise,' she said, 'hello.' My gin bottle caught her eye.

'Some of us are meeting in Ronan's room to have a couple of drinks before dinner. Can you join us?' I lifted the bottle up. 'Do you like gin? If not, Gil has bourbon.'

'I can drink gin,' she said. 'Come on inside.'

Blanche's berth was no different from mine, a single bunk squeezed into a tiny space. She'd stretched a cord between the bulwarks. A slip, two pairs of panties and a pair of stockings hung drying from it. She ducked under it and beckoned to me. 'I know the bed's not tidy, but there's room for both of us,' she said. We sat cross-legged on the bunk among blankets, her coat, purse and an open book. A pack of cigarettes and a lighter rested on the pages.

'It's good of you to ask me to join you,' Blanche said. 'I know you're trying to be nice. But I don't want to be anywhere near Gil. I' – and here she paused, her lips tightening and anger flaring in her eyes – 'I can't stand the man. He's the one who spreads all the gossip about me. I want to be left alone until we get to England. I only want to go home and live with my family again. I married Eddie because he was a rich American and I've paid enough for that mistake.'

So Blanche didn't love her husband even before he was injured. That was a strike against her, but was it a motive for murder? If she'd come upon him alone at the ship's rail, all she had to do was open the gate and push him through it.

'Look,' she said, picking up a framed photograph from the bedside shelf and handing it to me.

I knew the photo was pre-war, because none of the men in it were wearing uniforms and

144

Blanche, the youngest of the group, was a teenager. 'My father and mother,' Blanche said, pointing the figures in the photo out to me, 'my sister, brother and me. My brother and sister have since married and I have two nieces. None of them believe I killed my husband.'

'I understand,' I said. I didn't like Gil much myself. I moved to get off her bunk, but she put a hand on my arm to restrain me.

'Do you think . . .' she said, hesitating.

'What?'

'That I could have some of your gin even if I don't go to the party? I could use a drink myself.'

'Sure,' I said. 'I've got nothing to add to it, though – not even an ice cube.'

'I've saved an orange; I'll add a slice to it.'

I poured her a double into her tooth glass. She opened the little drawer under the shelf next to the bunk and pulled out an orange. I noticed several napkin-wrapped bundles inside, evidence that Blanche was still taking leftover food from the mess. So odd. But then she was an unusual woman. Most people, no matter how unhappy they were, didn't rebuff every single offer of companionship or vanish for hours at a time, even during a gale.

I'd forgotten to bring some of Dellaphine's pralines to take to the party, so I stepped back into my cabin. From where I stood, I saw Blanche leave her berth, but she didn't spot me. She was wearing her coat and hat, carrying her glass of gin, and had a napkin-wrapped bundle under her arm. She hurried to the staircase, clearly not wanting to be seen. Where on earth was the woman going? She acted as if she was planning

145

to meet someone – hence the gin. Had to be Tom, despite the rules against fraternizing with passengers. He wasn't on watch, so he was probably waiting for her in one of the vehicles strapped to the deck of the ship.

I almost didn't care anymore; I was tired and confused by my suspicions about Grace's death. I had no facts at all to go on, other than that her corpse didn't look as if she had fallen, and that wasn't enough.

I rapped on Ronan's door and Gil opened it. 'Come on in,' Ronan said. I stepped in and crawled on to Ronan's berth with Olive.

'Did you get any rest?' Olive asked.

'Some,' I said.

'A drink or two will cure what ails you,' Gil said, handing me a glass he'd filched from the cafeteria. I uncorked my bottle and poured an inch into my glass, while Gil served Olive and Ronan from his freshly opened bottle of bourbon. I sipped my gin and gratefully felt it wash through my body and numb my brain.

'Poor Grace,' Olive said.

'She's beyond pain now,' Ronan said. 'And life is full of suffering.'

'Yes, it is,' I said. 'Life can be very painful indeed. I want to think Grace is at peace.'

'Do you doubt it?' he said.

'I don't know. I hope you're right.'

Ronan raised his glass. 'May the Lord take a liking to you, Grace Bell,' he said.

Gil broke the somber silence that followed. 'I take it Blanche isn't joining us,' he said.

'Nope. She's got other plans,' I said.

146

'What do you mean?'

'I poured her a drink in her berth,' I said. 'But then I saw her head up the stairs wrapped up in her coat and scarf with the drink in her hand.'

'Think she's meeting someone?' Olive asked.

'I have no idea,' I said, 'but she moved like she had a plan.'

'She is an attractive woman,' Ronan said, 'and had an unhappy marriage. It wouldn't be a surprise if she was interested in a new man.'

'She's been seen with Tom Bates, the Navy ensign,' Gil said, 'and they were friends on the voyage over.'

Olive and I didn't say we'd seen them together. Gil would be sure to tell the entire ship if he knew.

'Let's not gossip about Blanche,' I said.

'Agreed,' Olive added. 'That's why she doesn't mix with us. She knows we're all talking about her behind her back.'

'There's not a lot else to talk about,' Gil said. 'Being on this ship is like living in a cave in Nepal. No newspapers, no radio, no movies, nothing. And with Grace gone, we'll get a lot less ship gossip.'

Grace did like to talk. It was from her that I first heard about Blanche's husband's death and the speculation that she'd murdered him.

The proverbial lightbulb lit up my brain. Who else did Grace gossip about? Did she talk as freely with the other passengers as she did with me?

'Servants will talk,' Gil said, as if he could read my thoughts.

'She wasn't a servant,' Olive said. 'She was a stewardess in the merchant marine.'

147

Gil shrugged. 'Small difference,' he said. 'She cleaned our rooms, made our beds and brought us coffee.'

'My niece worked in a stately home before the war,' Ronan said. 'Owned by one of our British overlords. She was the upstairs maid. You wouldn't believe what she knew about her employers. To them she was just a piece of furniture.'

I poured myself another drink. 'Most of us didn't think of Grace that way,' I said.

'Maybe not. But she still saw everything that went on,' Ronan said, 'and I mean everything.'

The lightbulb in my brain was still burning bright. Was it possible that Grace was murdered because of something she'd seen and gossiped about? Something she didn't realize was dangerous? I filed the thought away to examine when I hadn't been drinking.

Blanche and Tom came into the dining room together. But when they carried their trays into the wardroom, they sat at separate tables – Tom with the master and the rest of his officers, and, to my surprise, Blanche with Olive and me.

'Don't say it,' Blanche said. 'I ran into Tom in the passageway.'

'We weren't going to say anything,' Olive answered.

The chief cook must have wanted to cheer up the crew after Grace's funeral. We had steak for dinner. A real one, not molded from hamburger. Mine was pink, just as I liked it. And a baked potato, peas, fresh yeast rolls and butter. Dessert was chocolate cake. It was delicious. I could hear the conversational hum grow louder, even some laughter from the seamen's mess next door. Olive didn't eat her baked potato, and I swear I saw Blanche staring at it. Surely she wasn't going to take a cold potato to her room!

While we were drinking our after-dinner coffee, the chief steward came over and asked us to join him at the Smits' table. We did so, taking our coffee with us. 'The thing is,' he said to us once we were seated, 'with Grace's death, well, we don't have a room stewardess for the women passengers. I'm not sure what to do – it's against regulations for a male steward to serve women.'

'*In's hemelsnaam*,' Mrs Smit said. 'We can take care of ourselves, can't we, girls?' she said to her daughters.

'Sure,' Alida said. 'I can draw my own bath.'

'Of course,' Blanche said, 'we can do everything ourselves. It's just tidying up and changing sheets and towels. Don't worry about us.'

Olive and I concurred. I could tell the chief was relieved, poor man. 'I can give one of you the key to the steward's closet,' he said. We agreed that Mrs Smit should keep the key with her and we would ask her for it when we needed it.

I stopped by our uncleared table to pick up my purse before leaving the wardroom, and I'll be darned if Olive's leftover baked potato wasn't missing from her plate. Blanche must have filched it when we moved to the Smits' table. What a strange woman.

I lingered on the deck alone after dinner. I needed to clear my head. I was out of practice drinking

149

gin. The night was clear for once, though freezing cold, of course. I rewrapped my scarf to cover most of my face to keep my nose from going numb. Countless stars wheeled overhead. They weren't very different from the ones I grew up with on the Carolina coast. I recognized Perseus and Ursa Major and Minor.

I was still feeling a bit tipsy when I went inside the superstructure. It was too cold to stay outside for long. Alone in the passageway, I passed the doorway to the utility room where Blanche supposedly rode out the gale, and where we joked that she spent the time she wasn't around.

On an impulse I reached out to open the door to the closet. It was locked. I stood there thunderstruck, with my hand still on the lever. I tried to open it again: still locked. A colored messman came by and spoke to me. 'Ma'am, that door is always locked. Do you need something? It's just got mops and such inside. I'm not on watch or I could have opened it for you.'

I dropped my hand. 'No, thanks, I was exploring a little bit. You know, now that Grace is gone, we'll be taking care of ourselves downstairs.'

'I think you'll find the steward's closet on your passageway will have everything you need,' he said. 'If not, just ask one of us.'

I thanked him and went on my way, rather robotically, toward the stairs, my brain absorbing this new information. Blanche had not ridden through the terrifying gale in that utility closet. Where was she and why did she lie about it?

* * *

I couldn't sleep that night, despite the gin and a big dinner. What I'd learned during my years at OSS kept me from accepting the master's decision not to order a formal investigation of Grace's death. It wasn't that I didn't understand why he made it: he had crushing responsibilities, commanding a cargo ship loaded with ammunition across the Atlantic Ocean in the dead of winter. A ship in constant danger from German submarines and airplanes. I could even understand how he could insist that Grace's death was an accident, even though we couldn't quite understand how it happened. And why would anyone have wanted her dead? About all I could come up with was her reputation as a gossiper, that perhaps she heard or saw something that someone was afraid she would talk about. But I had no evidence of that. And how on earth could we place anyone at the scene, when the ship's crew and passengers were on deck gaping at an iceberg? It would be impossible to establish alibis for everyone.

But I'd been taught to solve problems, not ignore them because they were difficult. I turned on my bedside lamp and rummaged in my purse for the stick drawing I'd made of the scene of Grace's fall. I just didn't see how she could fall down the stairs but with her tray and its contents landing in the passageway. Gravity and the stair rail made that impossible. And if she'd fallen all the way down the stairs, why were there no bruises on her body? Her only injury was the awful head wound that killed her. The scenario that fit the scene – which I *could* visualize

151

– would be if she had been in the passageway, and someone had crept up behind her and hit her hard enough to kill her. Her tray would fall to the passageway floor. Then her killer would arrange her body to look as if she'd fallen down the stairs. All while most of the ship's crew and passengers were on deck.

First, I needed to establish the time of Grace's death. That was easy. Roughly four o'clock – the usual time Grace brought our afternoon coffee and cookies to us.

Now, alibis. Who had them? Olive and me. We were together at the ship's rail, gaping at the iceberg, at the time Grace died. So was the Smit family. Ronan was on the boat deck smoking and admiring the ice mountain. Then he spent a few minutes with Olive and me at the rail. Gil said he was on the boat deck with Ronan and joined Ronan at the rail while he finished his pipe. Tom stood with me and Olive for a bit, then left to tell Sparks to broadcast the coordinates of the iceberg to the rest of the convoy. I needed to check that out, but I was fairly sure it was correct. Tom could hardly shirk that duty.

Then there was Blanche. Where was she? She claimed to have been on the boat deck during the iceberg spectacle. I'd check that with Gil and Ronan. Cautiously. I didn't want them to know what I was doing.

That accounted for the casual passengers, except for Blanche. What about the rest of the crew? I thought I could exclude most of them. They hardly knew Grace.

Could Grace's death possibly have something

to do with Eddie Bryant's? She did gossip about it . . . could she have known more about his death than she realized? Could his killer have murdered her to keep her quiet? This narrowed the suspects down considerably. Most of the crew on the *Amelia Earhart* hadn't shipped on its previous voyage, so I could eliminate them.

Who was on that voyage? Starting with the victim, Eddie Bryant, a paralyzed American Air Force pilot disabled when his plane crashed. By all accounts, he was unlikeable at best, a man so angered by his fate that he lashed out at everyone around him. Including his wife, Blanche, who disliked him in return, and who spent very little time with him – didn't even pretend to play a devoted wife. Instead, she played cards and smoked on the deck with Ensign Tom Bates, who commanded the Navy Armed Guard. He was young, handsome and perhaps interested in Blanche, since Olive and I came upon them in an isolated jeep on deck during this trip. Then, of course, there was Grace, a sweet young woman who liked to gossip. She was the stewardess on the first trip across the Atlantic and was in a good spot to know the goings on among the civilian passengers. She had occasionally sat with Bryant so his orderly could take a break. Then there was Gil Fox, a salesman from the American Rubber Company, who tried and failed to befriend Bryant. Like Grace, he had implied that Blanche had had a good motive to kill her husband. And Nigel, Bryant's orderly, who inexplicably left Bryant alone near the ship's rail while he looked for a lighter. Who fell in love with Grace.

The merchant mariners on board who'd made the trip from England were the master, who'd refused to conduct an official inquiry into Grace's death, Chief Popeye and Chief Pearce. A few others maybe, whose names I didn't know.

If I was going to look seriously into Grace's death on my own, I needed to know where everyone had been when she died – when the iceberg had interrupted the ship's routine. And I couldn't take anyone's word for it; I needed corroboration.

This was the master's job, but he wasn't doing it. So I would.

I would either make a fool of myself or find a murderer.

Eleven

'Don't you want some syrup?' Olive asked.

'No, thanks,' I said. 'I like jelly on my pancakes.'

'Why on earth?'

'Syrup gets all over everything,' I said, as I spread strawberry preserves over my pancakes, preserving the integrity of my ham.

Without Grace to keep us organized, the civilian passengers had straggled into breakfast. We gathered into our usual groups. I came in last, joining Olive, while Blanche ate with the Smits family, and Gil and Ronan sat with Tom.

'Want some coffee?' Olive asked.

'Sure,' I answered. I was logy from lack of sleep and needed to wake up.

Olive poured us both cups of coffee and pushed the cream and sugar over to me.

I drank half a cup, then forced myself to eat.

'It was so odd not to hear Grace's knock on my door this morning,' Olive said.

'And her singing,' I said. 'Her voice made getting out of a warm bed bearable.'

I did feel better after coffee and some food. We sat over a second cup; there wasn't much else to do.

'Listen, Olive, I've decided to do something and I need your help.'

'If it passes the time until lunch, I'm willing.'

155

'No, it's important.' I lowered my voice. 'I want to investigate Grace's death.'

'Oh, Louise, no!' Olive said, rolling her eyes. 'Dearie, you have to put that behind you. There's nothing to be done.'

'There's nothing to be done because she wasn't murdered, or because we're helpless to do anything about it?'

Olive studied her coffee and didn't answer me.

'Come on,' I said, 'you know as well as I do that Grace's death is suspicious. I just can't forget how unlikely her fall was.'

Olive looked up and met my eyes. 'I know. I remember how unmarked her body was. Not what you would expect from a fall down a metal staircase, even a short fall. But what can we do?'

'I think we need to verify some alibis,' I said.

'Of everyone on the ship?' Olive asked. 'That's impossible.'

'No, just the individuals who knew Grace best. The civilian passengers, the master and his officers, Tom, Nigel. Remember what Gil said the other night? As a stewardess, Grace knew what went on with all of us, and she'd been on previous voyages with some of the others. Murders aren't random – whoever killed her had a motive.'

The Smits passed behind us on their way out of the nearly empty wardroom. We stopped talking until they passed us by. I noticed Tom leaving, too. It must be close to eight o'clock, when his usual watch began. As he passed by Blanche, their eyes met and they shared brief smiles.

'Did you see that?' Olive asked. 'Tom and

156

Blanche? I'm not surprised, after we caught them sharing that jeep, remember?'

'I remember,' I said.

Ronan and Gil left then, probably on their way outside for their first smoke of the day.

Now that we were alone, Olive and I could talk more freely. She was thinking along the same lines I was.

Olive whispered, 'Do you think Blanche or Tom – or both – could have killed Eddie so they could be together? And then murdered Grace?'

'Anything's possible, but we don't have any real evidence yet. That's why we need to establish alibis first. You and I were standing at the ship's rail during the excitement over the iceberg, when Grace died. So we alibi each other.'

'Grace brought us our coffee like clockwork, at four o'clock,' Olive said, 'so the murder had to happen then. The Smits were with us, so they have alibis, too.'

'Yes, and I can't imagine why they would harm Grace anyway. Blanche told me she was on the boat deck. Did you see her?'

'No, but I did see the master on the bridge deck.'

'Me, too. He's in the clear. But we have to find someone who saw Blanche.'

'Ronan and Gil were together – most of the time anyway.'

'We still need corroboration if we're going to do this properly.'

'OK. And Tom, of course.'

'He told me he was going to see Sparks about

157

broadcasting the iceberg's coordinates, so we'll need to check that out,' I said.

'Are you sure that we need to check on the officers?'

'I am. Except for the chief engineer; I can't imagine he has anything to do with this. But Chief Popeye and Chief Pearce were on the voyage when Eddie Bryant died. Chief Pearce knew Grace very well – he was her boss. Even if they aren't suspects, they might know something important.'

'And Nigel? Do you think he could have killed his boss?'

'I guess he could have. Why did he leave Eddie alone to go in search of a cigarette lighter? Surely one of the seamen could have lent them a light. And he could have pushed Eddie overboard and then made up the story about the lighter. But he didn't kill Grace. He was on the boat deck all the time she could have been killed. I saw him there myself.'

'I don't like this at all,' Olive said. 'I don't want to think any one of these people is a killer.'

'I don't either,' I answered. 'Maybe we'll find out they are all innocent. I hope so.'

The view from the deck didn't change much. Gray sky, gray ocean, gray ship, other gray ships in the gray distance. Chunks of ice floating in the choppy sea. Seabirds following, screaming, waiting for the kitchen refuse to be dumped overboard. Seamen bundled in foul-weather gear, black watch caps pulled over their ears, doing their endless chores. I longed for light and color, but I expected that London was gray, too. And spring was a long time away.

I found Sparks doing what most of the men did on their breaks, leaning on the rail of the ship, smoking.

Sparks, who, like most enlisted men, was just a skinny kid, touched his cap to me. Maybe he was twenty-two or twenty-three. Maybe. He offered me a cigarette.

'Thanks,' I said, 'but I don't smoke.'

He nodded and went back to smoking himself. 'Are you glad to be going to England, ma'am?' he asked me.

'I am. I've always wanted to go abroad. Of course, it's during wartime. But still. What about you?'

'For sure,' Sparks said. 'We'll have some shore leave. I'd love to see a play, if they're putting any on these days. I've read all of Shakespeare's plays.'

'Really!'

'Yep. I was in college training to be an English teacher when the war started. If I don't get blown up, I intend to finish.'

'That's why you read so much.'

'There's not much else to do, ma'am.'

'I guess the iceberg gave you something to do,' I said. 'Ensign Banks told me on the deck he was on his way to tell you to broadcast its coordinates to the convoy.'

'Yes, ma'am,' he said, tossing his cigarette butt into the sea. 'But he didn't tell me himself. He sent one of the gunners to me with the message.'

My gut clenched. I'd expected Sparks to verify

159

Tom's alibi. I'd assumed he was innocent. Why? Because he was handsome and likeable? During my time at OSS, I'd met plenty of handsome, likeable, evil men. And women. It was hard for me to imagine that Tom might have killed Grace to cover up Eddie Bryant's murder, but I had to add him to my suspect list. Unless he could come up with another alibi.

Olive was accustomed to uncomfortable situations. She'd been a nurse for ten years, part of that time during this war. She'd seen death, tragedy and suffering and learned to live with it. But she'd never investigated a murder before. Louise had told her to pretend she was an actress, to play a part. Engage people in casual conversation, then pry their alibis loose. All she had to do, Louise said, was get Ronan to corroborate Gil's alibi – that they were on the boat deck together when Grace was killed. Olive wasn't used to snooping. She was surprised that Louise was. She was just a file clerk. When did she learn how to nose around like this?

Olive found Ronan in the wardroom playing solitaire at one of the tables. She went to the 'entertainment' closet to look for a book, where she found an Armed Services edition of *The Grapes of Wrath*. She'd read it already, but she was only going to use it as a prop.

'Can I sit here and read?' she asked Ronan. 'I'm so tired of my berth. I can get another table if you'd rather be alone.'

'Of course not; I'd be glad of your company,' he said. He threw down his cards and then

160

gathered the entire deck to him. 'I can't seem to get a good run here,' he said.

As Ronan reshuffled, Olive noticed how worn and scarred his hands were. 'What did you do before you retired?' she asked.

'I was a bricklayer,' he said. 'It paid the bills and I liked the rhythm of it. I'd rather work – the days are so long without it – but I'm just too old. I put a bit of money aside; I hope it's enough. That's why I'm going back to Northern Ireland – I can live with my sister.'

'I know what you mean. I miss my job, too. I'm eager to get to my next posting. Thank goodness for books. I've managed to find enough to read.'

'I've never read much except the newspaper. Maybe I'll take it up when I get to Bridget's.' Ronan dealt himself new cards and leaned over them, pursing his lips. 'Looks like I have a better hand here.' He began to flip his cards and stack them.

Olive thought this might be her opportunity to pry.

'We need some excitement,' Olive said.

'I reckon a German submarine would be exciting, but I'd rather be bored, thank you!' Ronan said, looking up from his game.

'Oh, I meant something like the iceberg!'

'That was an astonishing experience. I'll never forget it.'

'I think you and Gil had a better view from the boat deck than we had from the rail,' Olive said.

'I don't know; you were much nearer to it. When I joined you there, it looked magnificent.'

So, Olive thought, that verifies that Gil and

161

Ronan were together on the boat deck. Mission accomplished!

'I didn't stay up there for long,' Ronan said. 'Too cold. That's why I joined you and Louise. After you left Gil came down from the deck and smoked a cigarette with me while I finished my pipe.'

There wasn't nearly enough time between when Ronan left the boat deck and when Gil joined him at the rail for Gil to have murdered anyone. Olive was pleased with herself. She'd gotten verification of Gil's alibi from Ronan. They were both in the clear.

After Olive left him, Ronan gathered his cards up again. 'I wonder what that was about,' he muttered to himself.

I didn't know how to go about checking Blanche's alibi. She'd said that she was on the boat deck, gawking at the iceberg, when Grace died. The boat deck was small compared with the main deck, but it was packed with crewmen off watch trying to get a good look at the berg. Gil and Ronan were up there, too. Olive had told me during lunch that their alibis held up. What was I supposed to do? Start asking everyone if they'd seen Blanche on the boat deck with them? That wouldn't be suspicious or anything! I couldn't ask Ronan; he'd already been quizzed once today. And Gil was so shifty that I didn't want to alert him to what I was doing; he was bound to make something of it. I'd seen Nigel on the boat deck myself, but I didn't want to bother him. He would still be grieving.

Didn't Ronan mention he'd talked to Popeye about the height of the iceberg? Popeye was on the bridge deck. So Popeye had an alibi.

Then I had an idea. Although the chief mates were always on duty, this wasn't Popeye's watch. Really, I should call the man Chief Pitts, but I couldn't get over the sight of his massive forearms. I was familiar enough with the ship's routine to be fairly sure where he was.

I climbed the metal ladder to the boat deck, clinging to the rungs while a frigid wind did its darnedest to blow me off. I should have made this ascent through the superstructure, but I was feeling so shut in that I wanted to be outside.

Sure enough, I found Popeye sitting on a camp stool near one of the lifeboats poring over a map. As if he was intent on navigating even when he wasn't at the wheel.

'How are we going?' I asked.

'Steady on,' he said, looking up at me and smiling.

I perched on a spool of rope nearby.

'Why aren't you inside?' he asked. 'It's freezing.'

'It's always freezing. I had cabin fever. And I'm tired of playing cards and I believe I've finished every readable book on board.' I quickly added, 'I'm not complaining, mind you. No news is good news.'

'No, we've had more than enough bad news for one trip,' he said, grimacing. 'Poor Miss Grace.'

'Yes,' I said, 'we all miss her terribly.' Then, changing the subject, I gestured toward the map. 'Can you show me where we are?'

He turned the map toward me, spreading it flat

on his knee. It was covered with navigational marks I didn't understand, but he pointed to a spot roughly two-thirds of the way to England.

'How long until we reach Liverpool?' I asked.

Popeye rolled up the map. 'A week to ten days,' he said, 'depending on the weather and the Germans.'

My heart clutched. We'd be on land soon, off this huge explosives-packed vessel, a clear target for submarines and airplanes. England wasn't what you would call safe, but it would be safer than this. I felt relief swell over me, but then reined it in again. A lot could happen in a week.

'Chief,' I began, remembering not to call him Popeye to his face and pulling my notebook and a pencil out of my pocket. 'I'm thinking of writing a story. About the iceberg. Just a small article I might be able to get published in a magazine.'

'Really?' he said. 'Sure. I've never been interviewed before.'

'Even if I can't get it published, it will pass the time. I've always wanted to write.'

Popeye stretched his legs and re-crossed them. 'What do you want to know?'

'Ronan said you measured the height of the iceberg with some kind of instrument. Would you tell me about that?'

'I used an old-fashioned sextant,' Popeye said. 'It's been used for navigation since the seventeen hundreds. You can measure anything with it as long as you can, well, triangulate. I could see the top and the bottom of the iceberg from where I stood. I had one of the seamen measure, with a sounding line – it's old-fashioned, too – the

164

distance from where I stood to the base of the iceberg. It's not perfect – he had to throw the line out to the base of the iceberg near the waterline and estimate. Then I measured the angle of the arc from the top of the berg, which I calculated by viewing . . . well, if I had a sextant with me I could explain it better. Anyway, then you have the two distances of the legs of a triangle, and you can calculate the other one mathematically. In this case, it's just close enough for government work.'

'Oh,' I said, confused. 'That's so interesting. I'm going to have to look up sextants in an encyclopedia once I get on shore, I guess. By the way, I want to talk to as many people as I can, about their impressions, you know. Who else was on the boat deck? I know Ronan and Gil were there. I've already talked to them.'

Popeye mentioned several seamen I wouldn't know if I fell over them. And Nigel, whom I'd noticed myself from my spot on the rail.

'What about Ensign Bates and Blanche Bryant?'

'I didn't see Bates. Why don't you ask Mrs Bryant yourself?'

I was prepared for this. 'I missed her at breakfast and she's not in her berth or the wardroom.'

'Yeah, that woman is a loner, for sure. She must have a hidey-hole somewhere. No, I didn't see her.'

So Tom and Blanche still didn't have alibis.

I again fought the wind climbing down the ladder to the main deck. I had some sort of idea about trying to find Blanche and Tom together. I searched among the vehicles on deck, had several conversations with various seamen on cigarette breaks, but couldn't find Tom or Blanche, alone or together. Mind you, I didn't try to get into any of the trucks and vans – that would be too obvious.

Back in my bunk, wrapped up in every blanket I had, I read through my notes. I should feel successful, I told myself. I'd found – through a very clever ruse, I thought – that Tom and Blanche weren't on the boat deck during the iceberg episode. And Tom didn't carry his message to Sparks in person. But I didn't feel successful. I felt rotten. Was it really possible that one or the other of them, or both, had murdered Grace? I'd been obsessed with the possibility of murder ever since finding Grace's body, but now it felt real.

'What do we do now?' Olive asked. Olive had joined me on my bunk, where we were reducing my stock of Dellaphine's pralines.

'I think we should go back to the master,' I said. 'And tell him he must conduct an official inquiry into Grace's death.'

'But we don't know anything,' Olive said, 'not really. Just that we can't alibi Tom and Blanche. But this is a big ship with a hundred people on board. And dozens of places they could have been.'

'I know,' I said, 'that's the point. We can't interrogate every seaman and every passenger. We'd never get away with it. But the master can. He can order everyone on board into his cabin one at a time and ask them anything he wants. He can send anyone to the brig. A master is king of his ship.'

'There's no motive. We have no proof at all that Grace's death was related to Eddie Bryant's death on the previous voyage – or to anything else for that matter. Just suspicions.'

'The master can ask questions about that too. He can ask Gil what he and Eddie talked about when Gil visited him; ask Nigel what he overheard and what Grace knew. And ask Blanche where she was when her husband and Grace were killed.'

'But he called the police when the ship docked,' Olive said. 'Wasn't there an investigation then?'

'Not much of one. Just enough to provoke gossip about Blanche. Anyway, we can't do anything about that now. It's finding justice for Grace that I'm concerned about.' I snapped the top back on the tin of pralines.

Twelve

The master was livid. His face was scarlet and a vein in his forehead bulged. His wizardish eyebrows were knit in a straight line across his forehead. I thought the man might have a heart attack.

'What is wrong with you?' he asked. 'Why can't the two of you mind your own business? The Secretary of the Navy made a terrible mistake allowing women on military vessels. It's not natural!' He slammed his hand down on the tiny desk in his quarters.

'We can't ignore the facts,' Olive said.

'I decide what the facts are on this ship!' the master said.

'Please listen to us,' I said. 'We think a young woman might have been murdered.'

The master, who looked more and more as if he might be eighty years old rather than in his spry seventies, gave in. He listened. When we were done, he toyed with his pencil for a few minutes, then looked up at us, speaking more calmly than he had in a long time.

'OK,' he said. 'You tell me that you can't place either Ensign Tom Bates or Blanche Bryant during the time of Grace's death. That, in spite of the fact that almost everyone was on deck when we passed the iceberg. OK, then. Let's ask them where they were. Seaman!' he called out.

The seaman on duty outside the master's cabin entered.

'Sir?' he said.

'Please find Ensign Bates and Blanche Bryant and bring them here right away. If you have any difficulty locating them, shanghai some help.'

'Yes, sir,' the seaman said.

After the seaman left, the master swiveled his chair toward us. 'This may take some time. I don't believe Ensign Bates is on watch. You may wait on my bunk until they arrive. I have some paperwork to finish.' He swiveled back to his desk. Olive and I perched on the edge of his bunk. I felt like a child sent to sit in a corner for bad behavior.

Ensign Bates had such an innocent, perplexed look on his young face when he entered the master's office that my purpose almost failed me. He pulled off his watch cap and spoke to the master, but not before he stared at Olive and me. 'Master?' he said. 'You sent for me?'

'These ladies have some questions for you and Mrs Bryant. We are waiting for her to join us.'

'What is going on?' he said.

'Be patient.'

We all waited like mourners in a graveyard when the casket is late for its burial – and it's raining.

The seaman the master had sent for Tom and Blanche showed up at the door with Blanche.

When she entered the cabin, her expression wasn't surprised, but defiant. The master dismissed the seaman, which left the five of us crammed into his cabin.

'What is this about?' Blanche asked.

'I hesitated to call you in,' the master said. 'But I want this matter closed. Mrs Pearlie and Miss Nunn have some serious questions for you. They are convinced that Miss Bell was murdered, and since I refused to open an official inquiry, they have been doing some private detection.' The master's tone of voice was decidedly derisive, but I knew to keep my mouth shut about it. For now, anyway.

Both Blanche and Tom exclaimed, but the master raised his hand. 'Please,' he said. 'Wait. First, I want Miss Nunn and Mrs Pearlie to explain their suspicions.'

Olive and I were both well trained in our vocations, and I thought that our presentations were clear and professional. I described Grace's position on the staircase and where the contents of her tray were scattered. Olive went over the lack of bruises on Grace's body. I watched Tom's face. By the end of our explanations, he looked perturbed, but not guilty. Blanche was furious, but she didn't look guilty, or even frightened, either.

'That's disturbing,' Tom said, 'but what does that have to do with me?'

'Tom,' Blanche said, 'don't you understand? You and I are lovers. We murdered my husband; Grace knew something that implicated us, so we murdered her, too.'

Tom went as white as the ice that floated all around us. He choked out a response.

'What is wrong with you?' he said to me and Olive. 'How could you possibly think such nonsense!'

'There's nothing wrong with us,' I answered. 'We believe that Grace was murdered, and since we have no official help from the master, we are trying to get justice for her. We haven't been able to place either of you at the time Grace died. We want to know where you were.'

'I was standing next to you at the rail of the ship!'

'Not for long. You said you needed to deliver an order to Sparks in the radio room. But when I talked to him, he said you sent one of your gunners to him with the message.'

'For God's sake! I was pulled away by a problem with the stern anti-aircraft gun. A defective shell had jammed the mechanism. It took me and two of my men an hour to repair it. I can give you their names if it's necessary.'

'Good,' I said. I was pleased that Tom had an alibi. Despite my determination to find Grace's killer, I was relieved that Tom was in the clear.

That left Blanche.

'Mrs Bryant, we all know that you prefer your privacy. But you must tell us where you were around sixteen hundred hours on the day Grace Bell died,' the master said to her. 'And if someone can vouch for that.'

'All right,' Blanche said. 'I will produce my alibi. But I'll need to fetch it. You may send a seaman with me if you're afraid I'm on my way to throw myself into the ocean.'

'What do you mean, "produce"?' the master asked.

'You'll see.' With that, Blanche turned and left.

The master ordered the seaman on watch outside his door to follow her.

'What is that damn woman up to now?' the master muttered.

The few minutes that passed went by very slowly. The master fiddled with the paperwork at his desk. Tom leaned up against the bulwark, his arms crossed. He wouldn't meet my eyes.

We heard footsteps coming down the passageway.

'At last,' the master muttered, turning away from his work. A knock sounded at his cabin door. 'Come,' he said.

Blanche came in holding the hand of a boy who looked to be around fourteen years old. Only his face and hands were clean. The rest of him was filthy. The boy was skinny, had dirty blond hair that straggled below his ears, bright blue eyes and the kind of obstinate expression often seen on the faces of young people the news magazines called 'teenagers'.

'Here is my alibi,' Blanche said. 'Bruce and I were together on the 'tween deck during the entire time the ship was near the iceberg. We were looking at it through a porthole near the ladder to Hold Five.'

The boy stepped forward and stretched out his hand to shake hands with the master.

'My name is Bruce,' he said. 'I snuck on board your ship at the Navy Yard.' The boy spoke with an educated British accent.

'I'll be damned,' the master said. 'A stowaway!'

'Mrs Bryant found me after we left port,' Bruce

said. 'She's been helping me. She gave me blankets and food. She brought me a life preserver during the gale and stayed with me.'

So that's where Ronan's extra life preserver had gone. And the leftovers that Blanche took from our meals.

'And what,' the master said to Blanche, 'were you thinking? You should have reported this child immediately. His family must be worried sick!'

'My family is in England,' Bruce said. 'They sent me to the United States to be safe. I don't want to be safe! I want to go home! Mrs Bryant understood and wanted to help me.'

'I took care of the boy until we were past any place you could drop him off,' Blanche said. 'I know how it feels to want to be home so desperately.'

'Ensign Bates,' the master said, 'would you please take our stowaway to the chief steward. See that he is cleaned up and fed. And we need to find him a bunk.'

'Yes, sir,' Tom said, taking the boy by the arm and guiding him out into the passageway. But not before Bruce winked at Blanche.

That left the three of us – me, Olive and Blanche – alone with the master in his cabin.

'Mrs Bryant,' he said to Blanche, 'once we reach Liverpool, I will see that you are charged with . . . I don't know what yet, but there must be laws against harboring stowaways. Believe me, I will find out.' He switched his gaze to Olive and me. 'Locking you up in the brig would be too good for the pair of you. You've disrupted the ship's routine, my work, irresponsibly, during wartime. Eddie Bryant killed himself. Grace fell and hit her head. There will be no more talk of murder – understand? Now get out of my sight.'

I hid out in my berth while the story of my humiliation spread around the entire ship. At least I assumed it was being passed from seaman to passenger and back around again. I must look like a fool. A bored spinster who invented a murder to occupy herself – the typical nosy woman.

Defeated by my failure, I'm sure the master assumed I'd be quiet and ladylike for the rest of the trip.

He didn't know me very well.

I dug my gin out of my musette bag and took a swig from the bottle and leaned back against the bulwark at the head of my bed. Yes, I'd been wrong, very wrong. Blanche didn't murder Grace. Neither did Tom. In a way, though, being wrong was well worth it, because I'd found out they both had solid alibis. Someone else had murdered Grace.

She had been murdered, I was sure of it, and no dismissal by the master could convince me otherwise.

I'd had visions of being completely ostracized by my fellow passengers and the ship's officers, but everyone was intrigued by our young stow-away and Blanche's role in his adventure. The two of them sat together at dinner, surrounded by the passengers and several of the officers, basking in the attention, like movie stars being

174

adored by their fans. The Smit girls, especially Corrie, peppered them with questions.

Bruce didn't say much at first. He was focused on eating a plate piled with meat loaf, mashed potatoes crowned with a chunk of melting butter, carrots and lima beans. The chief steward had done a good job cleaning him up. His dusty blond hair was revealed as straw-colored and he had light freckles spattered across his nose. He was wearing seaman's trousers cinched to his narrow waist with a rope and a thick sweater with arms rolled up.

'I did my best to keep him fed,' Blanche said, 'but I'm afraid he's lived mostly on apples and bread.'

'What would you have done if Mrs Bryant hadn't found you?' Corrie asked.

Bruce had excellent manners. He finished chewing and swallowing before answering.

'I was going to sneak out at night and steal from the galley. But like an idiot, I didn't realize the galley was just as busy at night as it was during the day,' Bruce said.

'How did you get on board to start with?' Ronan asked.

'The dock was so busy that no one paid any attention to me. I hid in a stack of cargo and got winched up with it. When it got lowered into the hatch, I crawled off at the 'tween deck. Otherwise, I would have been caught by the seamen unloading in the hold.'

'You must have been really cold,' Alida said.

'Yes, I was. But I found a bulkhead right next to the engine stack and made camp there.'

One of the messmen brought a second plate of food and offered it to Bruce. 'Still hungry?' he asked the boy. 'Want another helping?'

'Yes, please,' Bruce answered. He resumed eating, leaving the rest of the story to Blanche to finish.

'I was looking for a place to sit alone and smoke a cigarette in peace,' Blanche said. 'I remembered the 'tween deck from my earlier voyage. There's a small door and a ladder down to it under the bridge deck. I tripped right over Bruce. We were both scared to death and screamed bloody murder. It's a miracle no one heard us.'

'Isn't it kind of serious not to report a stow-away?' Mr Smit asked.

Blanche shrugged. 'After I heard Bruce's story, I just couldn't turn him in.'

'So, Bruce,' Tom said, 'I know you've been grilled by the master and Chief Pearce. But how about telling your story to the rest of us?'

Bruce shoved his empty plate away from him and shrugged. 'I want to go home. I hated being sent away with my sisters. Lots of boys my age are helping in the war effort. I could be a bicycle messenger, or work on a farm. What was I supposed to tell my friends? That I was safe in America while they were dodging bombs?'

'Where are your parents, then?' Mrs Smit asked.

Bruce shrugged again. 'That's the thing.' His voice cracked, which he tried to hide by finishing his glass of milk. 'I haven't seen them in ages. My father is in the army. He was in North Africa and now he's in Italy. My mother's doing

176

something secret with codes. She's jolly good at maths. I don't know where she is, but she's fine, my grandmother says.'

'So you were living with your grandparents?' Mrs Smit said.

'Yes, but we didn't see much of Grandfather, either. He was always at work. He was a professor of modern languages at Cambridge, but now he's in the Foreign Office.'

'That must have been hard on your grandmother,' Ronan said, 'taking care of you children on her own.' Blanche began to shake her head at Ronan, but he didn't notice.

'She was always a tough old bird,' Bruce said, 'until my uncle died. He was my father's younger brother. Grandmother, well, she had a rough time. Some days she didn't get out of bed. That was when my mother and grandfather decided to send my two sisters and me to stay with friends in America.' He cleared his throat. 'I'm going back home! I can help, and no one can stop me!'

Ronan laid a gentle hand on Bruce's shoulder. 'I can see why Mrs Bryant kept your secret,' he said. 'Of course, you should be home; you could be a big help to your family.'

Bruce blinked back tears. 'Thanks,' he said.

'Look,' Ronan said, 'has the chief steward given you a bunk yet? I'm in a double by myself. Want to share with me?'

'Sure,' Bruce said, 'that would be great.'

The sunshine brought us all out on the deck the next morning after breakfast. We knew not to delay; the weather could change at any moment.

We could even see some of our fellow convoy ships, no longer gray formless shapes surrounding us in the fog. Flags, mostly American or the Union Jack, fluttered from their staffs. The *Evans* was nearby, as usual. The corvette painted on its side was clearly seen in the sun.

'Do the Germans really fall for that?' Bruce asked me.

'It's convincing when the weather is as bad as it usually is,' I answered him.

Popeye allowed Bruce, Alida and Corrie to outline a shuffleboard court with chalk on the main deck. The three of them used deck brooms to shove shuffleboard cocks made from the lids of paint tins around, shouting with excitement. The sunshine and the sound of their fun lifted my spirits.

I sat on one of the wooden spools that littered the deck, leaning back against the bulwark of the superstructure, my eyes closed, enjoying the warmth on my face.

To my surprise, Blanche came and sat with me. I'd assumed she wouldn't have anything to do with me after my accusations.

'Oh, Blanche!' I said. 'I want to apologize to you for suspecting you and for creating that scene in the master's cabin yesterday. I had no business—'

'Nonsense,' Blanche said. She pulled her pack of Luckies out of her coat pocket and lit one with a gold cigarette lighter. I wondered if the lighter was Eddie's. 'You had every right to suspect me. I behaved badly. It was the same when my husband died. I already had a reputation as such a bad wife that the gossip that I might have killed him was perfectly natural.'

I was stunned to hear her admit that.

'I couldn't hide how unhappy I was, or how bad the marriage had become. If I'd had any sense, I would have avoided Tom completely, but I figured playing cards and listening to music with him was the last fun I would ever have. Once we got to the States, I'd be trapped with Eddie, living with him and his parents for the rest of my life.'

Bruce and Corrie crashed into each other on the makeshift shuffleboard court, but after disentangling they set up for another game.

'It feels like eons since I was their age,' Blanche said. 'I've made so many mistakes – well, maybe just one. But it was a big one.'

'What?' I asked. 'Marrying Eddie?'

'Indeed. I thought marrying him would be so exciting. I mean, I was virtually working as a barmaid in my parents' hotel, endlessly cleaning off tables and pulling beer. Eddie took me to dances at the American base, out to dinner, for rides in a friend's car. He said that after the war he could become a pilot for an airline and make real dough.'

'And then he had the accident?'

'Even before then I knew I'd made a mistake. He was self-centered and bad-tempered. But I had no choice but to return to the States with him. I wasn't sorry when he killed himself, and I suppose it showed.'

'So you do think he killed himself?'

'Yes, I do.'

'Don't you think it's a bit odd that Nigel left him alone to get a cigarette lighter?'

'Eddie's squadron gave him that lighter as a farewell present. This one, in fact,' she said, holding her lighter up. 'He kept it with him all the time. He'd want Nigel to find it right away. Then I guess he saw his chance to escape what he considered his miserable life and roll off the deck.'

'Where were you?'

'Smoking a cigarette at the other end of the ship. Alone. No alibi. But no one saw me anywhere near Eddie either. Of course, the master had to report Eddie's "suspicious" death when we arrived in port. I didn't exactly look at it that way, but I was sure he suspected me. Then, of course, I booked my return journey home on the same bloody ship, with some of the same people, all of whom had nothing to do but gossip about me.'

'You did rather vanish, you know,' I said. 'We all thought it was quite suspicious, that you were avoiding us. We couldn't figure out where you were – you were never in your berth.'

'You thought I was making out somewhere with Tom, right?'

'Well, the notion that you were caring for a fourteen-year-old stowaway didn't occur to us.'

Blanche held out her hand to me. 'Truce?' she said.

'Truce,' I answered, accepting her hand.

'I'm off your suspect list, then?' she said.

'Definitely.'

She stubbed out her cigarette butt on the deck.

'From what little I know of you, I'll bet you're still wondering about Grace.'

'I can't help it,' I said. 'The facts don't fit an accident.'

'Maybe you don't know all the facts yet?'

'That's what Olive said.' I didn't think Olive was completely convinced that Grace's death was an accident either, but we were both stymied. All the passengers and crew who knew Grace before this voyage had alibis, and I couldn't imagine why anyone else would want her dead.

'I've been wondering something,' I said. 'How did Eddie get up on deck? He was in a wheelchair.'

'His arms were strong. He would hang on to the stair rail and pull himself up while Nigel carried his legs. Then he'd sit on the floor at the top of the stairs while Nigel got the wheelchair. When we boarded the ship, the crew winched him up with one of the davits.'

If it hadn't been such a clear, sunny day, the seaman on watch in the bow wouldn't have seen the torpedo headed our way. Nor would the ship have had enough time for any response at all.

The siren sounded just as the shout of 'Torpedo!' rang out from the seamen ranged along the rail of the starboard side of the bow. 'All hands on deck!' blared out from the bridge loudspeaker and the ship's crew appeared from every nook and doorway of the ship, running in organized confusion toward their battle stations. The noise from the siren, orders shouted and commands from the bridge deck was deafening.

A seaman grabbed Blanche and me by the arm.

181

'Get to the lifeboats and stay there. Tell the others if you see them. Stay out of the way.' Blanche collared Bruce and the Smits had their girls. We ran to the boat deck where the lifeboats were rigged, dodging seamen who ignored us as we ran by. We gathered next to our designated lifeboat. Ronan joined us, then Gil and finally Olive. The ship shuddered as it veered sharply to starboard, throwing us to the deck, where we stayed huddled together. Below us, two seamen began to winch down the accommodation stairs so we could climb down into the lifeboats once they were launched. Thinking of the munitions stored in the hold, I doubted we'd have that chance if a torpedo hit.

'They can blow up the torpedo with the deck guns, can't they?' Bruce asked. He was squeezed between Ronan and Blanche, who each had an arm around him.

He was too old to lie to.

'The twenty-millimeter guns aren't powerful enough to detonate a torpedo, even if they could hit it,' Gil said. 'And the anti-aircraft guns aren't angled properly. They'd just blow a hole in the deck.'

'Don't worry, lad, half the time these German torpedoes are duds,' Ronan said. 'Feel how sharply the ship is turning? The master's trying to evade the torpedo. He wouldn't be doing that if he didn't think it might work. We'd already be in the lifeboats.'

The *Amelia Earhart* wasn't making her sharp turn gracefully. She groaned and creaked, and I thought of the tear in her deck from the gale.

And the lack of rivets in her construction. I could visualize the ship pulling itself in half under the stress of its maneuvers, although I supposed that would be easier to survive than a torpedo hit.

The *Evans* was the closest vessel to us. We could see it across our bow, far too close to us than seemed reasonable. 'She's trying to get clear of us so she can take a shot at the last known location of the sub,' Gil said, reading my thoughts.

'That submarine will have long left its position by now,' Ronan said. 'They must be tracking it on sonar.' Which wouldn't help us survive one bit. The torpedo would hit us any second, I thought, unless we managed by some miracle to escape.

How much time had gone by? How fast was a German torpedo? It seemed so long since we'd first heard the alarm. I stood up to peer over our lifeboat. A clutch of seamen had gathered at the bow, gesturing to Popeye on the bridge deck to keep the ship moving to starboard. The torpedo must be close, very close.

Even though the guns were supposed to be of no use, I could see Tom and several of his gunners crowded around the gun position at the bow. Tom held a small crate under one arm and a hand grenade in the other. Even I knew that was ridiculous. You couldn't stop a torpedo with a hand grenade, even if you did manage to hit it.

Blanche pulled me back down.

'Listen,' Gil said to us all. 'The women and children will need to load the lifeboat before any general evacuation can happen. A seaman will go down the stairs first to help us board. Mrs

183

Smit, I suggest that you carry Corrie down the staircase next, followed by Alida and Bruce, Olive, Blanche and Louise, then Mr Smit, Ronan and me. The seamen assigned to our boat will follow and we can launch, and the rest of the crew can abandon the ship.'

'I'd like to stay behind,' Olive said, 'there may be injuries.'

'Ma'am,' Ronan said, 'you'll have a much better chance of helping any injured men if you get off the ship right away.'

I thought this was an excellent plan, but unlikely to be successful. And I wished I had eaten up all the pralines.

When the explosion came, it wasn't as loud as I expected, but had a muffled, thick quality. The ship responded by lurching even farther to port, throwing us all up against the boat deck rail. The seaman standing there, waiting for an order to abandon ship, caught Alida before she slid on to the staircase. Then, instead of bursting into flames and continuing to tip to port, the ship righted itself, rocking on heavy swells. I felt the engines slow and the ship almost seemed to breathe in relief.

'*Godzijidank*,' Mrs Smit said, clutching her daughters. Ronan pulled a crucifix on a chain from under his shirt and kissed it. I remembered the good luck charm Milt had given me and patted it through my life preserver and multiple layers of clothing.

Then came the next, much louder, explosion. Corrie screamed, and I covered my ears to protect them from the pain. The munitions, I thought. We were done for, after all.

But the *Amelia Earhart* just rocked in the turbulent ocean that followed the explosion.

'I'm going to find out what's happened,' Gil said. 'Stay here, I'll be right back.'

But we all got to our feet anyway, eager to see what was going on. Bruce pulled out of Blanche's grasp and scaled a ladder halfway up to the bridge deck. 'I don't see any fire or anything,' he shouted down to us. 'Everyone on deck is cheering. I think the torpedo missed us!'

Mrs Smit began to sway, so Olive helped her sit back down. I felt shaky myself. I remembered what Winston Churchill once said – 'Nothing in life is so exhilarating as to be shot at with no result' – and understood it perfectly.

'But I think the torpedo hit the *Evans*,' Bruce said. 'I can see fire and smoke billowing out of a hole above the rudder!' In the distance, we could hear the sounds of alarms from the ship.

'Are they abandoning ship?' Ronan shouted up to Bruce.

'No, I can see seamen on deck with fire hoses,' Bruce answered.

Gil returned, elated with excitement and relief. 'You won't believe it,' he said. 'Our ship was evading, but it still looked like the torpedo would hit. But Tom had a box of grenades at the gunner's station. He pulled the pin on one, put it in the box with the others and threw it into the ocean between the ship and the torpedo. The explosion knocked the torpedo off course!' It hit the *Evans* instead, but it doesn't look like there's much damage there.'

'I've never heard of such a thing,' Ronan said. 'What were the odds that would work?'

'Did the grenades damage our ship?' I asked.

'The chief engineer has a crew over the side already looking,' Gil said. 'The master told me we need to stay here for a while longer until we're sure the ship is still seaworthy.'

'What about the *Evans*?' Bruce asked.

Chief Popeye appeared on the ladder from the bridge deck, forcing Bruce back down.

He raised his fingers to his lips. 'We require absolute silence now for the listening gear. We're trying to locate the submarine. Stay here until I tell you otherwise.'

We huddled together on the deck near our assigned lifeboat, trying to stay warm. We were out of the wind, which was something, but still freezing and getting very hungry.

After a couple of hours we sent Bruce up on the ladder to report on what was going on below. 'I can see the rope ladders over the sides where they're inspecting the skin of the ship,' Bruce whispered. 'Especially near the bow, where I guess the grenades exploded. And there are chaps lining the rails with those microphone things that hang over the sides, and headphones, listening.'

The second mate arrived with a message for us from the master. We were to go to the wardroom and pick up a cold dinner, then return to our berths. 'Stay fully dressed and wear your lifejackets,' the man said. 'Be absolutely quiet. Don't even whisper. We're still trying to find the submarine.'

The last thing we saw before we headed below

186

was the sloop HMS *Robin* passing by us faster than our ship could dream of, her deck stacked with depth charges.

In the wardroom we picked up sandwiches and apples, carrying them back to our berths. It was good to be alone, tucked up in my bunk, where I didn't have to be brave. My heart still pounded with fear and my nerves were shot. My hands actually shook as I ate my ham sandwich. I could hear small explosions in the distance, and I wondered if they were depth charges detonating, and if that meant the sloop had found the submarine. By now the sky outside my porthole was pitch black, with an occasional flash on the horizon. I didn't expect to sleep, but the next thing I knew the sky was lightening into dawn. I sponged myself off at my tiny sink and changed into the only clean clothes I had. Maybe later today I could get a real bath and a shampoo, and hand-wash what laundry I could.

Breakfast was cold – cereal and toast – as I'd expected, but I wasn't very hungry. Mostly I wanted coffee. After I'd drained two cups, I went out on the deck. I found Olive and Blanche leaning on the rail, peering over the side of the ship.

The sea was full of debris, most of which I couldn't identify. Pieces of sheet metal and jagged wood planks floated on the light swells. What appeared to be cushions, chairs and crockery drifted together like rafts. I noticed at least one suitcase and one life preserver – empty, thank goodness.

187

'It's all from the *Evans*,' Olive said. 'But the torpedo just glanced off it. It's dropped back in the convoy to make repairs.'

'Did anyone die?' I asked.

'Not that we've heard,' Blanche said, 'but the sloop and the other escort destroyer chased the submarine all night. Tom said the RAF would send planes up today to keep searching. Either for the sub or a debris field.'

'So the sloop and the destroyers aren't nearby, then?' I said.

'Nope,' Olive said. 'We've got a few corvettes for protection.'

A group of seamen up toward the bow of the ship were winching up a set of ropes as thick as their arms, following orders shouted from below. A platform carrying Chief Popeye and several seamen appeared at the rail and was hauled over the side on to the deck.

'There's a dent in the side of our ship from the grenade explosion,' Olive said. 'Those men went down to check all the welds.'

'Tom seemed really surprised at breakfast that the box of grenades diverted the torpedo,' Blanche added. 'He said he did it out of pure desperation. Then he was afraid he'd blown a hole in our hull. He didn't look as if he'd slept much last night,' Blanche said.

Blanche and Olive went back to the wardroom for coffee, but I walked the length of the ship. I needed the exercise. And stupidly, I suppose, I wanted to see for myself that the *Amelia Earhart* was seaworthy. I didn't want to go down with this ship just a few days out from Liverpool!

I found the chief engineer and several of his men working on the tear in the deck that had opened during the gale, which felt as though it had happened months ago. The tear extended through the patch several feet at both ends, now stretching halfway across the main deck of the ship. The engineers were busy riveting sheets of metal over the now rather frightening wound.

'The stress from the sharp turn the skipper made to evade the torpedo caused the tear to expand,' the chief engineer said, seeing me standing nearby with a hand to my heart. 'As long as the ship doesn't experience any more structural stress, we should be OK.'

'I thought all those stories about Liberty ships splitting in half were jokes,' I said.

'They had to build them so quickly,' he answered, 'I expect most of them will be scuttled after the war. They weren't built to last long.'

'What about the dent in the bow?' I asked.

'The hull is sound,' he answered. 'Ensign Bates is lucky. If he'd blown a hole in the ship, or if anyone had died on the *Evans*, he could have been court-martialed. Instead, he'll probably get a medal.'

A cheer went up on the deck and a couple of men pointed out a cluster of black dots in the sky that grew into a formation of fighter planes.

'The RAF,' a seaman said. 'Bless them.'

'We'll be seeing more and more of them now that we're getting closer to land,' the chief engineer said.

A rectangle of ocean to the west of Ireland was thick with German submarines and the infamous

189

Luftwaffe, trying to pick off Allied shipping as it neared port. We were probably more in danger now than ever. I would be happy when the *Evans* and the *Robin* returned to their stations.

I admit that my questions about Eddie Bryant's death and Grace's death, which I still suspected was a murder, receded into the back of my mind. I figured I'd done everything I could. Now I just wanted to get to shore and walk off this ship alive.

Thirteen

The master stood up at his table and tapped his glass with his knife. The room quieted. I noticed that Popeye left the table and opened the wardroom door into the seaman's mess so the seamen could hear him.

'Gentlemen,' the master said, and then he nodded in our direction, 'and ladies. As you know, since the US Navy has taken over wartime command of the merchant marine' – he nodded at Tom – 'for which we are eternally grateful, of course' – at which we all chuckled, including Tom – 'this ship has been dry as a bone.' We heard boos from the mess next door. 'However, the master of a ship, from time immemorial,' he continued, 'has been allowed to bring in a supply of his own drink for special purposes. I have not failed to honor this tradition.' There was absolute silence next door. 'So tonight there is beer for all!' Thunderous applause commenced from the mess. 'Two bottles for every man not on watch, and for the watch when it comes off duty,' he said. 'And, of course, for the civilian passengers if they are so inclined.' At that point the door from the galley opened and two messmen pushed in a rolling tub packed with bottles of beer nestled in ice.

We were so inclined.

* * *

191

After the tables were cleared and the first bottles were opened, someone brought out the record player and records from the storage cabinet in the wardroom. After just a few minutes of toe-tapping, and definitely after second beers were breached, dancing began. All those salty rough seamen didn't hesitate to take to the floor and dance with each other! The six women passengers, though two were underage and one was married, didn't lack for partners.

We lindy-hopped and jitterbugged to Glen Miller, the Andrews Sisters and Duke Ellington. Mrs Smit retired early, but the rest of us carried on. Bruce and Corrie stayed together, learning the steps from Alida and Blanche. When the watch changed, new seamen arrived to drink their beer allotment and ask us to dance. We were hot for the first time in weeks, removing our outer clothing and heavy socks. I found myself dancing with Popeye in my stocking feet, ruining one of my pairs of hose.

I took a break, waving off yet another dance. I was exhausted, but in a good way. I heaved myself on to a table next to Tom, who was breathing heavily from tossing Blanche around the dance floor. Blanche was still out there, jitter-bugging with two seamen and showing no sign of slowing down.

I glanced around. 'Where are Gil and Ronan?' I asked.

'I don't think they fancied dancing with each other,' Tom answered. 'They went out on deck to smoke, I believe.'

'Those two have gone through a lot of tobacco,' I said.

'There's not much else to do if you're not working,' he said.

'I think Olive and I have read every book on board. Even the Westerns.'

'Despite the gale and a submarine attack, this has been a fairly uneventful crossing,' Tom said. 'Except for Grace's death, of course.'

Grace's death. It looked more and more to me as though we'd never know whether her death was an accident or a murder. I supposed I'd just have to walk away from my certainty that there'd been foul play. There wasn't enough evidence to push for an inquiry. There was no consensus about how she fell. No clues at the scene. No sign of a murder weapon. No motive, either, except for my own niggling thought that her death might have been related to Eddie's. And everyone who knew Grace on that previous voyage had an alibi.

I wasn't used to failing to solve a problem. I didn't like it, but I might have to let this one go.

I noticed Nigel slumped in a corner nursing his beer, watching the dancing. From his expression, I figured that his friends had given him some of their beer ration. Poor fellow.

I got to my feet and waved off a couple of seamen who wanted a dance. 'I'm going to go outside and cool off,' I said to Tom.

With my coat, socks and shoes back on, I went on deck, where the frigid air assailed me, sending chills down my sweaty body. I welcomed the cold; it woke me up and countered the effects of my two bottles of beer.

I saw Ronan and Gil inspecting two tangled

193

airplanes on deck. One had broken free from its mooring during the evasion from the torpedo and slid into the other. They were a mess of bent steel. The undercarriages of both had collapsed.

I went down to the deck and joined the two men.

Ronan stood puffing on his pipe, watching Gil crawl around under the planes.

'Do you think they'll push them overboard?' I asked. The planes looked totaled to my inexperienced eye.

'No,' Ronan said. 'The master decided not to. They might be repairable once we reach England, maybe. The Allies need every piece of military equipment they can get.'

Gil was on his hands and knees examining the ruptured tires of one of the planes.

'Goodyear,' he said, dusting off his trousers and hands. 'At least it's not mine. Nobody can sue me for this.'

On my way back to my berth I was waylaid by a couple of seamen who wanted me to lead a conga line. No one else would do, it seemed, so I did my patriotic duty and went back to the mess. Only Alida and I were left of the women to take charge of the dance. The two of us bopped around the mess hall followed by a long line of men intently watching our hips move. But they behaved like gentlemen, and Alida and I had a lot of fun snaking along to Xavier Cugat's Cuban beat.

Alida didn't want to leave the dance, but I

insisted. I was exhausted and I knew the Smits wouldn't want Alida to stay alone at the dance.

'I'm eighteen! Almost, anyway!' she protested.

'And I'm thirty,' I said. 'Do you want me to wake up your father so he can come up here and get you?'

'No,' she said. Reluctantly, she followed me down the next ladder and then to the head of the stairway to our hall. We both paused, struck by the steepness of it, both thinking of Grace.

'One hand on the rail and the other on the bulwark,' I said.

'I remember,' Alida said, 'I'm not a child.'

Grace wasn't a child either; she was the one who warned us about the stairs, and yet she had fallen. Or at least that's what her family would be told.

Silently, the two of us moved downstairs. There were no sounds from below, so I supposed that everyone else was asleep. At the door to her berth, Alida turned to me, hesitating.

'What is it?' I whispered.

'Are you really thirty?'

'Yes, I am,' I said.

'You don't look that old,' she said.

'Thanks heaps,' I answered.

'You have time to get married again,' she said. 'Don't you want to?'

'If I meet the right man,' I said. 'Otherwise, I'm happy to stay single.' Alida looked at me incredulously, as if I might be certifiable, then went on into her berth.

In my own berth, after I undressed to my long underwear, put on clean socks and drew on flannel

195

pajamas, I pulled Joe's picture out of my bedside drawer and wondered if I'd ever see him again. Although he had a British passport, Joe was Czech. If he survived the war, he'd most likely head home immediately to find his family. Then what would he do? And how quickly would I be discharged by OSS and sent back to the States? I had no idea.

In the middle of the night I awoke with a start. I sat up, sure that something had woken me. I had been sleeping deeply, worn out from dancing, and I heard something. Didn't I? But the night was quiet except for the steady thrum of the *Amelia Earhart*'s three vast engines. Sure that I'd heard something, I got up, wrapped a blanket around my shoulders, went to the door and opened it. Looking out, I saw nothing but an empty passageway. The air was silent. Everyone must be asleep, as tired as I was from the evening's festivities.

I climbed back into my bunk and checked my watch. It was almost four o'clock. The watch bells would be sounding soon. I'd gotten so accustomed to them that I rarely noticed them.

When the bells sounded, I was still wide awake. This was unusual. Once I was asleep, I almost never woke in the night. I was tired. My body ached. I wanted to go back to sleep in the worst way, but my mind was busy. I turned on my light and helped myself to one of Dellaphine's pralines. I tried to trick my brain by pretending I didn't want to go back to sleep. I was fine lying here awake. If I didn't sleep again until morning, what did it matter? I had nothing to do. I could stay in my berth all day and nap if I wanted.

I started awake again. My light was still on. I had the same feeling that something had woken me up, but this time I remembered a snippet of a dream. I was watching an airplane crash, spiraling downward like ones I'd seen in newsreels, wondering if the pilot would escape by parachute. In my dream he didn't. The plane hit the ground with a terrible noise and burst into flames. Then the scene changed, and I saw the plane's wreckage, piles of metal still smoking. That scene shifted to Gil poking about the wreckage. He kicked both of the airplane's tires. That was when I woke up. And I knew that this was the same dream that I'd had earlier in the night, even though I didn't remember it then. Something about it niggled at me. Even though it was early, I got up. I went down the hall with an armful of dirty clothes and drew my bath. I soaked in the hot water for a few minutes, then washed my hair for the first time in several days. When I got out of the tub, I wrapped myself in a towel and set about doing my laundry. I washed my smalls, a couple of pairs of socks, a set of long underwear, the two shirts I'd worn for at least a week and my grubbiest pair of trousers.

Back in my berth, I dressed quickly in clean, or sort-of-clean, clothes. I dried my hair as well as I could with a hand towel. I hung my laundered garments out to dry on a cord I'd strung from the handgrip next to my bunk to a hook on the opposite wall. It would take at least a full day for everything to dry, longer for the trousers.

It was an egg day. I took my plate of egg, toast and bacon into the wardroom and joined the Smits family. That egg tasted excellent. I looked forward to the day when I could have two. Probably not until I returned to the States – although the Brits ate eggs, fried potatoes and sausage for meals other than breakfast, didn't they? I could hope.

After the others had left, I stayed behind with Mrs Smit. I had a second cup of coffee while she sipped on another cup of tea.

'That nice young ensign says the ship will dock in three, maybe four days,' Mrs Smit said. 'Although there is still much danger.'

'I feel like I've been at sea for a year,' I said. 'Imagine sleeping in a real bed!'

'I cannot.'

'Where will you and your family live?'

'I don't know,' she said. 'The Dutch government will find us a place. As long as it has two bedrooms, a bathroom and a cooker, we will be fine. It will be hard on the girls. We rented a big house in California. But my husband is so happy to be called to work for our government in exile! He felt helpless after we fled to the States.'

'Like Bruce,' I said.

'Yes,' she said. 'We all want to serve in some way. Perhaps this terrible war will end soon? Bram thinks an invasion is planned.'

I knew that invasion was coming, but my OSS training kicked in and I said nothing about it.

'I hope so,' I said.

198

'Where will you live?' she asked.

'In London,' I said. 'But I'll be lucky to get a bedsit.' Another boarding house would be more likely.

I covered a yawn with my hand.

'You didn't sleep well?' Mrs Smit asked.

'No, I had a recurring dream that woke me up twice. This is silly, but I think it meant something. I just can't figure out what.'

'My *moeder* used to say that our minds solve problems while we sleep, in our dreams. Sometimes we have to wait for the meaning to become clear.'

I had the same three options I'd had every day since I left DC on the *Amelia Earhart*. I could go back to my berth, climb into my bunk and wrap myself up in blankets to stay warm. I could stay in the wardroom and try to recruit someone for a game of checkers or cards. Or I could go out on deck, where the temperature was near zero, wander around and watch the seamen at work.

I found a deck of cards in the storage cabinet and counted them to make sure there were fifty-two. Then I dealt myself a solitaire hand. I'd always had an affinity for clubs when I played cards. Too bad they were the least valuable suit.

Suit. That word struck me. Suit. Lawsuit. Lawsuit! I remembered that Grace had told me that Eddie Bryant complained constantly about the crash that crippled him. He'd said the crash wasn't his fault, that something was wrong with the plane itself, that he was going to sue the responsible party as soon as he got to the States.

199

What was it Grace had said? 'Who was he going to sue? Hitler?'

Yesterday when Gil and Ronan were looking at the two wrecked planes on the deck, Gil had gotten down on his hands and knees to inspect the ruptured tires. Then he'd expressed relief that the tires weren't made by his company because then he couldn't be sued. Was it possible that Eddie had planned to sue Gil's company?

It was a long shot. Most likely a coincidence, and certainly circumstantial. Who might know more about Eddie's crash? I couldn't talk to Gil; he'd be warned off. And he had a hard and fast alibi for Grace's death. But my OSS training couldn't be silenced. This was a loose thread I had to tie off before I could put my mind at ease. Who else might know more about Eddie's crash and tires and such? Nigel, since he had spent so much time with Eddie. And Blanche. She'd know the most about Eddie's plane crash. Both Nigel and Blanche had alibis for the time of Grace's death, too.

I gave up my game of solitaire and went out on deck. I couldn't say I was accustomed to the frigid temperature, but I was no longer shocked by it when I stepped outside. I simply wore two layers of clothes, my peacoat, watch cap, wool mittens and a scarf layered about my neck and face. As I stepped out on to the deck, I bent into the wind.

I found Ronan and Blanche sheltered from the wind behind a truck. The two of them were watching Bruce and Corrie play an intense game of jacks. I sat down next to them on a metal chest fixed to the deck. Blanche was smoking, as usual, while Ronan leaned back against the truck with his arms crossed. I was surprised to see him without his pipe.

'Have you given up smoking, Ronan?' I asked.

'No, I'm afraid I'm running low on my pipe tobacco. Didn't buy enough for the trip. Got to make it last,' he said.

'I offered to teach him to smoke cigarettes, but he seems to think fags are a lesser form of tobacco,' Blanche said.

'I'm not used to inhaling so deeply,' Ronan said. 'I don't like it.'

'I'm surprised any of you smokers have a voice left, the amount of tobacco you've breathed in on this voyage,' I said.

'There's not much else to do,' Blanche said. 'It's not like we can garden or sew. I wish I'd brought something to knit.'

'Or could go down to the pub for a pint of the black stuff,' Ronan said. 'Or listen to music on the radio of an evening.'

I was a failure at knitting but I sure wished I'd crammed more books into my luggage.

Bruce let out a triumphant yelp as he scooped up every last one of the jacks with one hand and caught the ball in mid-bounce with the other.

'Not fair,' Corrie said. 'Your hands are bigger than mine.'

'It's almost time for the galley to dump the garbage,' Bruce said. 'Let's go watch the birds and the dolphins fight over it. Maybe we'll see a shark!'

'Sure!' Corrie said. The two of them jumped

201

to their feet and headed aft. Ronan stood and stretched.

'I'll tag along with the chiselers to make sure they don't tumble into the drink,' Ronan said. He followed the two kids toward the ship's garbage chute.

'Chiselers?' I asked Blanche.

'It's Irish slang for kids,' Blanche said.

After a few minutes of silence, Blanche turned to me. 'Out with it,' she said.

'Is it that obvious?' I asked.

'Yes, go ahead and ask your questions,' she said. 'I have nothing to hide. I take it this is about Grace's death?'

'I'm afraid so. But it's Eddie I want to ask you about.'

'Whatever you do for a living, you're wasted. Unless you're a detective or something.'

I took that as a compliment.

'Grace told me that she sat with Eddie sometimes to give Nigel a break,' I said. 'Eddie told her that he hadn't crashed his plane, that something mechanical on the plane failed that caused the crash. And that he was going to sue the people responsible.'

Blanche shook her head. 'Poor Eddie. He couldn't accept that he was at fault for his accident.'

'What happened?'

'His commander told me that his approach to the airfield was off, and he landed at an angle, with just one wheel on the ground. The undercarriage disintegrated and the plane slid along the runway on its belly, causing a terrible fire. Eddie was pulled out of the wreckage just in time, but in the end he lost the use of his legs. His co-pilot died.'

'It must have been a terrible crash,' I said.

'It was.'

'What did Eddie think was wrong with the plane?'

'He wouldn't talk to me about it. He said I wouldn't understand.' She rolled her eyes. 'He'd never confided in me, and our marriage was breaking down even before the crash. After the crash it was over, except in law.'

'Thanks,' I said. I still had nothing to go on, except for a confusing dream.

'If you still want better answers, you should talk to Nigel,' Blanche said. 'He was with Eddie more than me, more than anyone. Perhaps he talked more to Nigel. Or speak to Gil. He tried to be a friend to Eddie, visiting him, offering to play cards, but Eddie would have none of it.'

The air-raid siren sounded, bringing both of us to our feet. We gripped hands, becoming close friends in fear. Then 'All Hands to Stations' blared. I could see the bridge deck from where we were. The master, Popeye and Tom crowded it, binoculars raised. The sun glinted off their lenses. Then we heard the sound of airplane engines approaching us. Some of Tom's gunners rushed past us, on their way aft to man the biggest gun on the ship, the five-inch cannon. The air-raid siren kept sounding, drowning out every other noise. Blanche had to lean over and speak directly into my ear.

'Corrie and Bruce!' she shouted.

'Ronan's with them!' I shouted back. 'We have to get below! Now!'

We struggled against a tide of seamen rushing to their stations. They ignored us to the point that one knocked Blanche down but kept running. I pulled her to her feet. When we reached the superstructure, we put our backs to the bulwark and edged along it until we reached the door.

'Bombs!' a seaman shouted as he ran past us. We looked up and saw death tubes falling from the sky. Our anti-aircraft guns blazed, their sound overwhelming even the siren. I paused for a second, watching the contrails soaring into the sky. I couldn't see Tom and the five-inch gun anymore – we'd moved too far forward – but the three-inch gun and the twenty-millimeter rapid-repeating guns fired relentlessly. Adding to the conflagration were the bigger guns booming from the *Evans*, and, in the distance, more gunfire from the other warships in our convoy. I'd seen battle footage in countless newsreels, and I'd survived a torpedo attack, but I wasn't prepared for the deafening noise and chaos of battle. I was afraid. In my mind's eye I could see all of us dead, floating in the ocean among the remnants of our ship.

The noise alone was enough to challenge one's sanity.

Blanche and I fell through the door. Ronan and the kids were there, flattened up against the outside bulwark. 'See?' Ronan said to Bruce. 'Here they are. We all need to get below!'

'Mama!' Corrie screamed. 'I want Mama!'

204

'Your mam will find you as soon as she can,' Ronan said, dragging her to the staircase.

'Wait,' I said. 'Don't go below!' If our ship got a fatal hit, our berths could become our coffins. 'We should stay above deck, in case we have to abandon ship,' I said. 'Head for the wardroom.'

'I'm going back outside,' Bruce said, with fourteen-year-old bravado. 'I want to fight the Nazis!'

'Oh, Mother of God,' Ronan muttered, grabbing Bruce by the waist and throwing him over his shoulder.

The rest of our company was already in the wardroom. Mrs Smit, sobbing, rushed over and hugged a tearful Corrie. Even Alida had tears streaming down her cheeks.

Gil stood at a porthole. He turned away from what he saw and slid to the floor. 'The sky is full of airplanes. And bombs falling. They look like bees swarming.'

An enormous explosion filled the air, rocking the *Amelia Earhart* with the concussive force of the blast. None of us could keep our footing, dropping to the tilted floor and sliding across it, slamming into the bulwarks. Something whizzed past us and pierced the bulwark. Then another one. It was pure luck that they missed us.

'Get under the tables,' Olive said. 'Hold on tight to the legs.' The metal wardroom tables were bolted to the floor, offering some security.

We waited, huddled under the wardroom tables, listening for the siren's signal to abandon ship. The order never came, and the ship righted itself.

Bruce crawled to the porthole and pulled

himself up. 'I think the bombs missed us and hit another ship,' Bruce said.

'Can you tell which one?' Ronan asked.

'No, there's too much smoke,' the boy answered. 'And now it's on fire.'

Mrs Smit muttered a prayer under her breath.

'Please don't let it be one of the destroyers,' Gil said. All the convoy ships had some kind of defensive weaponry, but only the two destroyers and the sloop were made for warfare. If we lost one, we'd be in dire shape.

The ten of us crouched under the metal tables of the wardroom, clinging to each other, afraid of imminent death. And all of us knew that the munitions our ship carried made our survival less likely. For the time we spent together crouched on the floor, we were the dearest of friends.

The cacophony of warfare seemed to diminish a little. Bruce pulled away from Ronan and scrambled over to a wardroom porthole. 'Wow,' he shouted. 'I just saw a plane crash! And another one!' Our anti-aircraft guns must have hit their targets.

Bruce ran for the mess hall before anyone could stop him. He made for the window, which was shaped like a large oval porthole. 'I see two ships sinking! And fire on another one!' he said. 'And there's just the tail of a plane sticking out of the ocean. There's a swastika painted on it!'

Ronan reached him and dragged him back to the wardroom. 'No wonder your parents sent you away,' he said to the boy. 'You're a handful!' He shoved Bruce back under the table, where Blanche gripped his arm with both hands to keep him there.

Then we heard a different humming sound. As if more airplanes were coming.

'You stay here,' Gil ordered Bruce. And he crept, staying low, into the messroom and over to the window. Then, to our horror, he crept along the bulwark and edged outside. A couple of minutes later he was back inside in one piece. 'Allied airplanes!' he shouted to us. 'Spitfires!' I didn't know I'd been holding my breath in, but now I let it out.

'The RAF, bless them,' Ronan said. We all crowded around the window to watch the Spitfires chase the Germans across the sky toward the mainland.

Fourteen

Our ship escaped a direct hit but it had been strafed several times. If the *Amelia Earhart* was a person, she would be one of the walking wounded. One of the cargo winches had been destroyed, collapsing across the deck, strewing busted metal parts, thick cables and struts across the width of the ship, damaging some of the vehicles underneath. Above me I saw that one of the twenty-millimeter anti-aircraft guns had been destroyed. There were two men down at the gunners' station. As I watched, another gunner, his face black with gunpowder and oil, covered the dead men's faces. The radio antenna had collapsed with the winch and hung over the side of the bridge deck, where I could see the master shouting orders from his bullhorn.

A team of seamen wielded hoses, putting out small fires fueled by oil spilled from the gun mounts and damaged vehicles. Water flooded the deck, making moving around treacherous. In this temperature it would freeze quickly.

I was relieved to see Tom on his feet, but his uniform was covered in blood. It couldn't be his blood, as he seemed unhurt. He and one of his men were inspecting the five-inch gun on the bow. Then they test-fired it. The sound made my nerves clang.

And everywhere – on the deck, on the vehicles,

on the side of the bridge, and on the bulwark of the level where the mess hall was – were holes and tears made by the German airplanes strafing us. Bruce had stood at the window of that mess hall, and Gil had actually gone outside; either of them could have been killed. Even a few of the lifeboats were punctured. And these holes were three times bigger than any bullet hole I'd ever seen – if you could call a three-inch-long projectile from a German aircraft cannon a bullet. Anyone who received a direct hit from one was a dead man. Including the two gunners who'd been brought down from the gun emplacement, there were seven corpses covered in tarps, lined up in a row on deck.

I would have given a month's pay for the emergency siren to stop blaring.

Only Olive and I were on deck. When the fighting stopped, the Smits took their girls down to their berth. Ronan and Blanche persuaded Bruce to leave, too. No one wanted the kids to see the hell on deck. Gil stayed in the wardroom to smoke. His hands were shaking so much that it took him three tries to get his cigarette lit.

Olive and I had this notion that we could help, but once we were outside, we stayed out of the way. It was too chaotic for us to even speak to anyone. Until we saw two stretchers carried by seamen coming toward us. The men on them were alive.

The pharmacist's mate gripped one end of a stretcher. He stopped when he saw us.

'Ma'am!' he called out to Olive. She immediately went to the wounded men. I followed her.

The first injured man had lost his left arm below the elbow. A tourniquet had stemmed the flow of blood, but his clothes were soaked with the blood he'd already lost. The second man lay on his stomach on the stretcher, unconscious. The back of his shirt was stiff with blood, too. It was Nigel.

'What happened to him?' I asked.

'Shrapnel in his shoulder, I think,' the pharmacist's mate said to me. 'Deep.' Then he turned back to Olive. 'Ma'am,' he said, 'I don't know what to do. There's a hospital on the *Evans*, but the launches are busy looking for survivors.'

'This man,' Olive said, taking the pulse of the seaman from his only wrist, 'won't live long enough to be moved anywhere. We have to do something now. Let's get him down to the first-aid room.'

The stretcher-bearers lifted the cruelly injured man on to the gurney in the first-aid room.

'What's his name?' Olive asked, rolling up her sleeves.

'Able-bodied Seaman Mike Oleson, ma'am,' another stretcher-bearer answered. 'I'm Seaman Andy Davis. He's my pal. Can you save him?'

Olive stared directly into the eyes of the pharmacist's mate. 'The only possible way to save this man's life is to take off his arm above the elbow,' she said. Already pale, the pharmacist's mate went ghost-white, gripping the edge of the gurney to stay on his feet. 'Pull yourself together,' Olive said to him.

'Yes, ma'am,' he answered. 'I can do it.'

'Do you have any plasma?'

'No, ma'am.'

'That's too bad. What's his blood type?'

The pharmacist's mate checked the man's dog tag. 'Type A, ma'am.'

Olive turned to the stretcher-bearer who was the injured man's friend. 'Andy,' she said, 'go find someone with type-A blood and bring him back here right away. Someone big and young. Don't let anyone stop you.'

'Yes, ma'am,' he said, leaving immediately.

Meanwhile, I was cutting the man's clothes off, finding a blanket to warm him and dripping water from a sponge into his mouth.

'We need anesthesia and an amputation kit,' Olive said. 'I sure hope you have them.'

'We've got ether and a kit,' the mate said, opening the storage cabinet door. But when he brought out the amputation kit and opened it, the collection of saws and knives sent a frigid chill down my spine. My legs felt as if they would give way. Olive noticed me sinking.

'Louise,' she said, 'go outside in the hall and sit down. Monitor Nigel. If his vitals change at all, call me.'

I tried not to stagger when I left the room. Just as I did, Andy came down the hall dragging a burly seaman with him and went into the first-aid room. I collapsed next to Nigel and took his pulse. It seemed steady to me, although he was still unconscious. The wound in his shoulder was small and circular. Maybe something like a bolt head had been driven into him.

Popeye came striding down the hall. He stopped

211

and knelt next to me. 'He OK?' he asked about Nigel.

'He seems stable,' I said. 'He has a piece of shrapnel in his shoulder. Olive is going to remove it when she's done with the other guy.'

'What other guy?' he asked.

'Mike Oleson,' the other stretcher-bearer said. 'His left hand and lower arm were blown off.'

'He's still alive?' Popeye asked. 'He didn't bleed to death?'

'No,' I answered. 'Someone got a tourniquet on him. Olive is going to amputate his arm. And his friend found a blood donor.'

'Good Lord,' Popeye answered. 'Does she know what to do?'

'Olive has been an operating-room nurse for years,' I said.

'Then I hope she succeeds. Seaman,' he said to the stretcher-bearer, 'you stay here. Anything Miss Nunn and Mrs Pearlie need, you find it for them.'

'Chief,' I asked, 'how many dead are there?'

'Ten, so far,' he said, 'and there are more bodies floating in the ocean. The *Evans* sent both launches to look for more, and survivors, if there are any.'

'The convoy?' I asked.

'Three cargo ships lost. And the *Robin*.'

An hour passed. It seemed to me that Nigel wasn't as deeply unconscious. When I spoke to him, he turned toward me, and once he opened his eyes.

The door to the first-aid room opened and the pharmacist's mate and Oleson's pal brought

212

Oleson on a stretcher out into the hall, followed by Olive wearing a blood-stained apron. Oleson was breathing. His lower left arm was missing and a massive bandage padded the stump.

'You did it!' I said to Olive.

'It's early days yet,' she said. 'Find a bunk for him,' she said to the pharmacist's mate. 'Take Andy with you. Keep a close watch on the patient. Any change and I want to know. If he starts to stir, he'll need morphine. Then see if he'll take some fluids.'

'Yes, ma'am,' the pharmacist's mate said.

The burly seaman who'd been commandeered to donate blood appeared in the doorway. He held on to the jamb. 'You took too much blood from me,' he said to Olive. 'I don't feel right.'

'Trust me, you'll live,' Olive said. 'Drink lots of liquids and rest for a couple of days. You'll make more blood.' She spotted the seaman that Popeye had left behind to help us. 'Help our blood donor to his bunk,' she said.

'Yes, ma'am,' he answered. 'But the chief said I was to stay here to help you and Mrs Pearlie.'

'Well, then, come back when you've finished.'

That left Olive and me in the hall with Nigel. 'Think you can help me carry the stretcher into the first-aid room?' she asked.

'Sure,' I said, 'he's skinny.'

Nigel opened his eyes. He lay on his stomach, his face turned toward me. We'd stripped off his shirt so Olive could clean the area surrounding his wound. Nigel winced. 'That hurts,' he said.

'Morphine coming up,' Olive said. She drew

213

liquid from a vial into a syringe. 'Here it comes,' she said to Nigel. She plunged the needle into the area near his wound. 'I don't think we're going to need an anesthetic,' she said. 'Once the morphine takes effect, I'll probe for the shrapnel.'

'Do you remember what happened?' I asked Nigel.

'Sort of,' he said. 'The chief had sent me to check the lifeboats for any damage from the strafing in case we had to abandon ship. I was halfway up the ladder to the boat deck when I felt something slam into my back. I lost my grip and fell. I woke up out there in the hall.'

'I'm going to probe now, so hang on,' Olive said. She inserted forceps into Nigel's wound and poked about. Nigel gripped the gurney and grimaced, but Olive was done already. She pulled a small rounded piece of metal out of Nigel's wound and held it up to the light.

'I'll be damned,' she said. 'It's a bullet!'

Fifteen

'What do you mean, a bullet?' It was impossible that Olive meant a round from a German aircraft gun. One would have gone right through Nigel and probably killed him. The smashed piece of metal Olive held in the forceps wasn't any bigger than a button.

Olive took the so-called bullet over to the sink and washed it off, then handed it to me, still secure in the forceps. I peered at it under the light that hung over the gurney. It was an actual bullet, all right – deformed, but still identifiable as such.

The meaning of this tiny bit of metal sank in. On a civilian cargo ship, such as the *Amelia Earhart*, operated by the merchant marine, no one was armed except the members of the Navy Armed Guard. The gunners were in the military; the seamen weren't. The Armed Guard manned the artillery and wore sidearms to be used in case the ship was boarded by the enemy. During an attack from the air, no gunner would have reason to use his sidearm. On this trip I only saw sidearms drawn when the gunners practiced shooting at a target buoy tossed into the sea.

I saw from Olive's expression that she was thinking the same thing. Someone had shot Nigel in the back during the chaos of the air attack.

Olive rummaged around in a drawer and found

a vial she handed over to me. 'Keep the bullet in there. We'll need to show it to the master after things settle down.' I secured the bit of metal in the vial and then tucked it into my bra. I had no intention of losing it. This bullet should prove to the master once and for all that there was a murderer on the *Amelia Earhart*.

Our two assistants, the seamen who'd help carry Oleson's stretcher and the one who'd escorted the blood donor, returned just in time to prevent Olive and me from having to carry Nigel to a bunk somewhere.

'The pharmacist's mate sent me to tell you that he's got Oleson tucked up in a bunk near the galley, and he ain't dead yet,' one of the seaman said. 'He wanted to know if you thought the other guy could get on to the top bunk? That way he could watch them both.'

Two bunks near the galley – that must be Grace's empty berth.

Nigel was sleeping like a baby from the effects of the morphine.

'I think so. Just be careful getting him up there,' Olive said. 'Tell the mate I'll come relieve him soon.'

Olive and I were left to clean up the bloody sheets and clothes and wash the used surgical instruments in the first-aid room.

The *Amelia Earhart* was full of holes, but none of her wounds were mortal. Two days after the air attack, the master, Popeye and the chief engineer agreed she was seaworthy and could continue on course. First stop, Londonderry,

216

where we would drop off Ronan, and then to Liverpool.

Ten of our seamen wouldn't be going on with us. One of them was seventeen years old. We gathered for their burial service and then all ten bodies were tipped into the cold sea. There were more dead from the three cargo ships and the sloop that were sunk by the Germans, but many of their crewmembers survived. The bodies of the dead and dozens of cold survivors were picked up by launches from the destroyers. We didn't know the exact number of the dead, but we could see white-shrouded bodies falling into the sea, like leaves falling in autumn, from the *Evans* during the burial service that took place shortly after ours.

Since the destroyers' infirmaries were packed, Mike Oleson and Nigel remained on our ship, cared for by the pharmacist's mate, Olive and me. Oleson would live – in fact, he was sitting up and slurping soup. Nigel complained about having to spend his days on his stomach. I rounded up some Western paperbacks to help him pass the time.

The trash on the deck was slowly cleared away. Seamen with acetylene torches dismembered the collapsed cargo winch and threw the metal remains into the ocean. When the cargo winch fell, it took the radio antenna with it, but Sparks was able to rig a replacement.

The vehicles we were transporting didn't escape damage. The collapsing winch dented jeeps and trucks parked under them. The German strafing left scars on others, including the locomotive.

217

The whole ship was pockmarked like a smallpox survivor. Engineers patched a few holes in the hull. But the tear in the deck didn't expand, thank goodness. It looked as if we would get to Liverpool in one piece. The chief engineer believed that much of the damage could be repaired once we docked.

We casual passengers, with the exception of Olive, who was busy caring for Nigel and Oleson and any number of other seamen with minor injuries, were respectfully requested to stay below and out of the way. Bruce was so restless, though, that the chief steward put him to work carrying coffee and sandwiches to the seamen working on deck. Olive and I decided to wait to tell the master that Nigel had been shot in the back with a handgun. He looked more and more frail every day.

I spent my time wrapped up in a blanket in my bunk, napping, snacking on Dellaphine's pralines and making notes about murder.

Sixteen

I wrote down every tiny detail I knew about Eddie Bryant, Grace Bell and Nigel Ramsey. My notes were many pages long and a disorganized mess. My conclusions that Grace, and possibly Eddie, had been murdered and that someone had attempted to murder Nigel were based on circumstance and instinct, which didn't amount to evidence. But I just couldn't let go.

Eddie may have been murdered or he might have killed himself. There were no witnesses to his death, and he had been strong enough to maneuver his wheelchair and propel himself overboard. Or someone could have come upon him alone, wheeled him to the rail and pushed him. I was sure that Grace was murdered, but all the casual passengers and crew who knew her had alibis. Nigel was shot in the back with a handgun. Could a gunner have accidentally discharged his sidearm during the melee of the German air attack? There was nothing to prevent a passenger, or another crewman for that matter, from bringing a handgun on board in their luggage, but all the civilian passengers were together in the wardroom during the attack.

I read through my notes again, organizing them and drawing arrows and circles around the facts that seemed important to me. When I was done, I realized that I needed to talk to Nigel.

Mike Oleson and Nigel had indeed been put up in Grace's old berth near the galley. The pharmacist's mate was delighted when I offered to sit with the patients for a time so he could get a cup of coffee and a doughnut.

Oleson was still quite pale from loss of blood, as you would expect, but he was sitting up in his bunk, with the stump of his left arm resting on a pillow.

'How are you feeling?' I asked.

'Better,' he said. 'I'm going to get solid food for dinner.' He glanced at his stump. 'I'm lucky I lost my left hand instead of my right,' he said. 'I can at least use a fork and spoon!' This guy had the right attitude, I thought; he would be OK.

'And you?' I asked Nigel. He was still lying on his stomach. Olive said she didn't want any pressure on his shoulder yet.

'I'm so bored,' Nigel said.

'Poor you,' Mike said.

'Hey, I'm going to go back to work in this damn war. They'll probably put you in some fancy hospital in a stately home where all you'll have to do is eat steak and chips and be waited on by pretty nurses.'

'Stop, both of you,' I said. 'I came to ask Nigel some questions.'

'Has anyone told you that you ask a lot of questions?' Nigel asked.

'Never,' I said. 'I've always been the quiet, unquestioning type. But what I want to know from you is whether Eddie Bryant ever talked to you about suing someone over his airplane crash?'

'I'm not supposed to gossip about my patients' conversations,' he said. 'That was beaten into us during training. A patient is entitled to privacy.'

'The man is dead, and, besides, Grace told me a little.'

Nigel sighed. 'I loved that girl, but she sure could talk. I suppose you're right, though: what difference does it make now? Eddie was positive it wasn't his fault that his plane crashed when he landed. He said he didn't land improperly, that the airplane's tires ruptured as soon as he touched down so he couldn't control the remainder of the landing. He was so angry! He said he was going to sue the company that made those tires.'

'Do you know what company it was?' I asked, trying to keep the eagerness out of my voice.

'The American Rubber Company – Gil's company,' Nigel said. 'Gil tried to talk to him about it when he visited, but it made Eddie furious and he refused to see Gil again.'

Finally, a motive!

'You left Eddie when you were on deck for a cigarette break – correct? You went back to his berth to find his cigarette lighter. That was when he died?'

'I shouldn't have left him,' Nigel said. 'But he kept that gold lighter with him at all times. I knew he wouldn't settle down until I got it. He'd dropped it when I helped him out of bed and it took me a few minutes to find it.'

'No one else was around out on deck?'

221

'Not a soul. Eddie was alone when I left him.'

Long enough for him to push himself through the gate in the rail, or for someone to come along and do it. Someone like Gil, who'd been smoking alone elsewhere on deck, he said. Or Blanche, who claimed to be doing the same.

'Does that help?' Nigel asked.

'Yes,' I said. 'It does.'

So I had two good motives for either Blanche or Gil to kill Eddie Bryant. Blanche, because she couldn't stand him or the thought of living with him for the rest of her life, Gil, because Eddie intended to sue the American Rubber Company. Except that both of them had cast-iron alibis for Grace's death: Blanche was with Bruce in the 'tween deck during the iceberg adventure, and Gil was with Ronan on the boat deck at the same time.

'My God,' the master said. He held the small lump of metal that Olive had removed from Nigel in his hand. 'It *is* a bullet!' He handed it over to Tom. 'Ensign,' the master said, 'could this be one of yours?'

I'd managed to convince the master to meet with me one last time. He asked Tom to join us. We were crammed once again into his cabin.

Tom examined the bullet under the master's desk lamp. 'No,' he said. 'It's too small. The Armed Guard carries Smith and Wesson thirty-eights. This is smaller. A twenty-two, I expect.'

'A derringer?' I asked.

'No, a derringer is loaded with one or two forty-five-caliber bullets,' Tom said. 'This came from a pocket pistol. It's a regular revolver, except smaller. It would load four or five bullets.'

'Small enough to be concealable?' asked the master.

'Definitely,' Tom said. 'Especially with the layers of clothes we've all been wearing. But a pocket pistol can be just as deadly as a full-sized handgun.'

'Olive said that if Nigel had been hit a couple of inches lower, nearer the heart and its blood vessels, he'd be dead,' I said.

The master sat on his bunk and rubbed his eyes.

'Well, Mrs Pearlie,' he said, 'I give in. You're right, I agree with you. The more I think about the issues with Grace's death that you brought up, the more suspicious I am that it wasn't an accident. And for one of my seamen to be shot in the back in the middle of an air attack! But I don't know what I can do about it right now. We can't possibly search the entire crew, the passengers and the ship for a pocket pistol. That's more than a hundred people. There are too many places where it could be hidden. I've got a cargo ship loaded with munitions to get to Liverpool and an exhausted crew. And I'm short of ten men.'

Tom turned to me. 'Do you still think that Grace's death and the attack on Nigel are related to Eddie Bryant's death?'

'I can't help but believe so – it's the only thing that makes sense. But the two people who might want Eddie dead – Blanche and Gil . . . well, there were no witnesses to Eddie's death. And they both have alibis for Grace's death. And Blanche and Gil were both with me in the wardroom during the air attack when Nigel was shot.'

'Remind me again why the two of them might have wanted to murder Grace?'

'Grace was a gossip. She told me all about Eddie's death and how the crew thought he'd been murdered by Blanche. Later she told me about Eddie threatening to sue Gil's company. I thought one of them killed her to keep her quiet.'

'And Nigel?'

I shrugged. 'I don't know. Except that Nigel knew that Eddie blamed Gil's company for his injury. And that Blanche and Eddie's marriage was a disaster. But, like I said, Gil was in the wardroom with the rest of us during the air attack.'

'Ensign,' the master said to Tom, 'I know you're stretched, but can you place a guard on Nigel? And on Mrs Pearlie?'

'No,' I said, 'not me. It would just draw attention to me. I don't want that.'

'But, Louise,' Tom said, 'I think it would be a good idea.'

'I don't,' I said. It would prevent me from learning anything else.

'You must promise not to be alone and to lock your berth,' the master said.

'I will.'

'I'll turn this over to the constabulary in Liverpool when we dock,' the master said. 'The passengers and crew will hate it. They won't be able to leave the ship until they're questioned and their belongings searched. We might not be able to unload our cargo right away either.'

Seventeen

Olive and I sat in the cab of the locomotive engine. It was pockmarked and had a cracked windshield, but other than that seemed undamaged. From that height we could see the expanse of the ship's deck all the way to the bow. The *Amelia Earhart* was battered but not broken. Sort of the way I felt.

Olive was smoking, of course. I was drinking the last of my gin. Straight out of the bottle! I'd told Olive everything that had gone on in the master's cabin when I showed him the bullet she'd extracted from Nigel's back. She deserved to know and I was sure she would keep her mouth shut.

'You see,' I said, 'this is a civilian American ship. The deceased were civilian Americans who died in international waters. That means the American FBI has jurisdiction over their possible murders.'

'But we're docking in England,' Olive said. 'In the middle of a war.'

'I know. So, instead, the master will have to contact the local constabulary, and they can call in Scotland Yard if they want.'

Olive stubbed out her cigarette on the floor of the cab and crammed her hands into her pockets. 'Does Scotland Yard have time for this?'

'No,' I said, 'and neither does the constabulary.'

225

Olive stared at me. 'Louise! You don't think anything will be done, do you?'

'No. There's just not enough evidence. The gun used against Nigel was probably tossed overboard. The crew and the passengers are desperate to get off the ship. The cargo needs to be unloaded, and the ship moved to dry dock for repair. The master told me the ship is scheduled to take German POWs back to the States in a couple of weeks. I expect the constables will take our statements and that will be that.'

'You seem awfully calm.'

'I've accepted it. There's nothing else I can do.' And I had accepted it. In a couple of days I'd be starting a new life. I hated that Grace would get no justice, but there were massive tasks to be undertaken to prepare for an invasion of Europe and I needed to clear my mind and concentrate on my new job. Grace's life was important, but thousands, millions, of other people's lives depended on the Allies' success.

The messman slopped the dreaded chipped beef on a burnt piece of toast, added a scoop of canned peas and carrots, for the third night in a row, and handed the plate to me. I plonked it on my tray with resignation. At least the rolls were still hot and fresh, even if we only had margarine to spread on them. Dessert was cherry gelatin. Over the course of the war I'd developed a pure hatred for gelatin. It was everywhere. The worse gelatin dish I'd been served was oxtail, carrots and parsnips suspended in gelatin made with chicken bouillon cubes. I swore I would never eat it again after the war was over. So I passed on the cherry gelatin dessert. I still had a few of Dellaphine's pralines left.

The casual passengers all sat together at breakfast. Despite the joy we all felt at the prospect of actually arriving at our destination in one piece, we were a somber group. We knew that an adventure was coming to a close, and that what happened to all of us next was likely to be much less interesting. And still so cold! Sparks had gotten a weather report from Liverpool that the temperature there was below freezing at noon.

I sat across from Ronan. He'd debark first. We'd drop him off at Londonderry the next day. No one would meet him, he said; it was impossible to notify his family when he was arriving.

'How will you get home?' I asked him.

'What?' Ronan said. He'd eaten little of his meal and looked as if he hadn't slept well.

'After you arrive tomorrow, how will you get home?'

'Oh,' he said. 'Bus.'

That was all he said. He looked unhappy to me, not contemplative or reflective like the others. No talk of Bridget and her grandchildren or anything else he was looking forward to upon finding himself back in his native country. He didn't even mention his first pint of Guinness. I noticed that he'd had rolled his tobacco pouch into a thin tube that stuck out of his vest pocket. There couldn't be enough tobacco left in it for one pipe. I noticed a tiny hole in the corner of the vest pocket, where the fabric was separating. The cuffs and collar of his shirt were frayed. I

227

didn't know how long it had been since he had laid a brick, but he still had heavy callouses and scars on his hands. I'd bet that his fare across the Atlantic had consumed a large portion of his savings.

Then a thought came to me that I badly wanted to reject. And couldn't.

'Ronan,' I said. 'Could we talk in private somewhere for a few minutes?'

'Sure,' he said, looking at me apprehensively. 'Of course.'

After breakfast the group broke up, Bruce and the Smit girls pulled a Monopoly game out of the storage cabinet in the wardroom. Olive and Blanche went outside to smoke. The Smits went down to their berth to pack. Gil came over and pulled a cigarette out of his pack, holding it out to Ronan. 'Ready to try one?' he asked Ronan.

'No, thanks,' Ronan said. 'I'm not that desperate yet.'

Gil shrugged and went on out of the room.

Ronan and I left the three kids playing Monopoly and went into the deserted crew mess. We took a table in the corner. Ronan picked up a salt shaker and turned it around and around in his hands. Then he put it back and met my eyes.

'Ronan,' I began. 'Please forgive me, but I must ask you a question that I'm afraid will make you very angry.'

'I lied when I said that Gil was with me when Grace died,' he said. He put his head in his hands. 'Oh, God, what a relief it is to tell the truth.'

His confession stunned me. Yes, I was going to ask if he'd lied, but having him actually say

228

so was painful. Ronan was a good man we'd all come to trust.

'Why?' I said. 'Why did you do that?'

Ronan sat up straight again and pulled the thin tube that was the remainder of his pipe tobacco out of his pocket, rummaged for his pipe and half-filled it. After he sucked the flame through the pipe bowl, he inhaled, then visibly relaxed against the back of the chair.

'It didn't seem like a bad idea at first,' Ronan said. 'Gil wasn't with me on the boat deck while we were all staring at the iceberg. He joined me later at the rail just as you and Olive were leaving. I finished my pipe while he smoked a cigarette. Then, on our way to the wardroom, we found Chief Pearce and Olive carrying Grace's body to lay out in the first-aid room. I was very upset, and Gil seemed to be, too. Then, after the stretcher passed us by, he asked me to say I'd been with him on the boat deck for the entire time I was there.'

'He asked you for an alibi.'

'It wasn't quite like that.' Ronan drew in another breath of tobacco smoke. 'He said he'd been involved in an earlier accident, the one where Blanche's husband Eddie killed himself, and his name had been in the newspaper. His company didn't like the publicity, and he didn't want to be involved in another mess. It didn't occur to me that he might have killed Grace. You have to believe me!'

'I believe you. But, Ronan, when Olive and I brought up the possibility of murder, why didn't you admit you lied for Gil then?'

'I still didn't suspect him of anything.'

'I believe that. Now tell me why you didn't explain what happened to the master.'

He didn't answer me, just sucked on his pipe and stared at the floor.

'Ronan,' I said, 'did Gil pay you?'

He lifted his head to face me. His eyes were wet with tears.

'Yes,' he said.

'How much?'

'Two hundred and fifty dollars.'

Money that would go a long way in rural Northern Ireland.

'You see,' Ronan said, 'I'm a poor man. So much of what I'd saved went for my wife's doctor bills and my passage home. But I'm afraid Bridget, my sister, is convinced that I'm a rich American. Oh, I have a little money, but I wanted to show up at my sister's door able to buy some treats for the family.'

'So, you accepted a bribe,' I said. 'You sold an alibi to Gil.'

Ronan flinched as if I had struck him. 'I still didn't believe Gil was involved,' he said. 'He kept telling me he might lose his job if he was involved in another death inquiry. Then, once Nigel was shot, I realized that Gil could have done it. And that made me wonder about him.'

'What do you mean?' I said. 'Gil was with us in the wardroom during the airplane strike.'

'Don't you remember?' Ronan said. 'Gil went into the hall to the door to the deck so he could see what was happening better. The ladder to the boat deck is right next to the door. I figured that

230

Nigel was climbing it just as Gil went outside. All the smoke and noise, Gil could have shot him then. I don't understand the whole story, but I know that Blanche, Gil, Grace and Nigel were all on the ship together when Eddie Bryant died and that the police were called in when the ship docked in New York.'

No, I hadn't remembered that Gil had briefly left the wardroom and I could kick myself for it.

'Do you know if Gil has a gun?' I asked.

'Yes, he showed it to me days ago. It's a little pistol, a handsome one. It has a carved bone handle and is engraved with his grandfather's initials. Apparently, the grandfather was a conductor on a railroad out west.'

'Ronan, you have to tell the master.'

Ronan had gotten all the smoke he could out of his half-filled pipe. He tapped the charred remnants of the burnt tobacco on to an empty butter plate on the table. 'I guess I will have to try one of those horrible cigarettes, after all,' he said.

'Ronan! You have to tell the master what you've told me! Right away! You're getting off the ship tomorrow!'

'No.'

'What?'

'I'm keeping the money.'

'You can't! You can't let a man guilty of murder go free.'

'You still don't know for sure that Gil killed Grace. Or shot Nigel. And nothing will bring Grace back. Once I get off this ship, I'm going straight to the nearest church to confess. God will forgive me, and I'll go home with money in my pocket.'

I could hardly breathe. He was right. And unless he broke his silence, Gil still had an alibi. Anything I could say about this conversation would be hearsay and Ronan could deny it.

The messmen had finished cleaning the wardroom and moved into the mess hall to clear the breakfast dishes away and set the tables for lunch. Soon we'd have no more privacy.

I had an idea.

'I understand about the money,' I said. 'My husband died during the Depression. I didn't have a penny. I had to move back with my parents. I hated it.'

'You're young and have a job now,' Ronan said. 'I'm past working anymore.'

I rummaged in my pocketbook until I found the gold coins that Henry had given me at dinner the night before I left DC. I dropped the two coins into my hand and reached out to Ronan.

'Take these. Then you can give Gil back his money and tell the master the truth.'

Ronan stared at the coins. 'I can't,' he said. 'I can't take your money. Are those coins gold?'

'Yes. And why can't you take them? You allowed Gil to bribe you. These are a gift. A friend gave them to me, and now I'm giving them to you. You can tell the truth and still take money home to your family.'

Please, I thought to myself. *Please*.

'I don't know what these are worth,' I said. 'On the black market, I mean.'

232

'Nowhere near two hundred and fifty dollars,' Ronan said.

Without hesitating I pulled the ring Phoebe had given me off my finger and added it to the coins on the table. 'I don't know how much this is worth either, but the diamond is real.'

Ronan stared at the coins and the ring for what seemed like a long time. He reached into his pocket and pulled out a battered wallet. He drew five fifty-dollar bills out of it and tucked them in his threadbare waistcoat pocket. I'd never seen a fifty-dollar bill before. Then he picked up the coins and the ring and tucked them into the coin slot of the wallet. 'I'll give Gil back his money right away. I wish I'd never gotten on this bloody boat.'

'No,' I said, 'no! You could be in danger if you tell him that you're going to tell the truth. The man has killed people, and he has a gun.'

'Then I'll find the master and tell him the truth first.'

After he left the table, I felt exhausted. Sweat trickled down my back as if I'd been running hard. I had a headache coming on.

But it looked as if justice might just win this one.

I expected that once Ronan had talked to the master, all hell would break loose. I needed a few minutes alone and some fresh air.

I walked the length of the ship. Once I got to the bow, I leaned over the rail and watched our wake churn for a few minutes. I gazed into the east, but as hard as I tried, I didn't see land yet.

I wondered if Ireland really was emerald green. Not this time of year, I told myself. Even Eden wouldn't be green in this weather.

'You witch,' Gil's voice said behind me.

I turned around and saw Gil standing very close to me. 'You witch,' he repeated. He raised his clenched fists to his chest. 'I should break every bone in your face,' he said, 'and then throw you to the sharks.'

My OSS training kicked in and I was immediately poised to defend myself. But how? My Schrade switchblade was still in my musette bag in my berth, where it had been during the whole trip. I had my hands and feet. Maybe there was something nearby I could use as a weapon.

But what had happened? How did Gil know that Ronan was going to the master to tell him the truth about Gil's alibi? And how did he know so soon?

'That ignorant Irishman told me he was going to give me up,' Gil said. 'He said that he'd talked it all over with you, you nosy female! Grace was the same way! Talk, talk, talk! And Ronan gave me my two hundred and fifty dollars back! What am I going to do with money on death row! I wanted to break his neck, but there were too many seamen around. So I guess I'll just have to break yours instead.'

'That won't help you,' I said. 'Ronan's on his way to tell the master the truth.'

'No, but it will make me feel good. Not as good as killing Eddie and that colored girl, but good.'

I needed to stall him, hoping help would miraculously appear.

'You killed Eddie because he threatened to sue your company,' I said. 'Is that right?'

'Damn right,' Gil said. 'I'd gotten a few complaints about those tires, but I didn't forward them to the company. If there was a lawsuit that might come out. I'd be fired and maybe charged with a crime. So a couple of airplanes had defective tires. Most of them didn't, and this is a damn war!'

'Why did you have to kill Grace?' I asked. 'She was such a nice young woman.'

Gil shrugged. 'She was a loudmouth. I thought she might gossip to someone who could put two and two together. And she did! You!' The menace in his voice and face was frightening. 'When everyone went nuts over the iceberg I saw my chance. I knew Grace would be coming down the stairs with the coffee tray soon. I hid in the lavatory. I heard her singing as she came down, and when I opened the lavatory door she'd just reached the bottom of the stairs and turned to go down the passageway. She never knew what hit her.'

'Why did you shoot Nigel?'

Gil shrugged. 'Who knew what that kid might have overheard? I had a chance to shut him up and I took it.'

He moved toward me. I had nowhere to go and no weapon. If I screamed, no one would hear me because of the noise of the wind and the ocean. I braced myself on the rail, determined to at least leave marks on his face where the others could see it.

'Cheerio, Mrs Pearlie! Hello, Mr Fox!'

Bruce! Oh no!

'Get out of here, kid,' Gil said. 'Louise and I are having a private conversation.'

'Miss Nunn sent me to find you,' Bruce said to me. 'She's trying to make a foursome for bridge.'

'You go on, honey,' I said to him. 'I'll be right along.' *Please go, Bruce, and be safe.*

Gil's jaw was working so hard I figured he must be cracking teeth. *Bruce, go*, I telegraphed to him with a warning look. Bruce telegraphed back, *No!*

'You heard the lady,' Gil said to him. 'We'll have our little talk and then follow you. Go on.'

Bruce had one hand hanging at his side, but he drew it up holding one of the big wrenches the seamen used to tighten or loosen nuts and bolts all over the ship. It was maybe twenty inches long. He tapped one end on his open hand.

'No,' Bruce said, defiant. 'Mrs Pearlie is coming with me. You do what you like.'

I was being defended by a skinny schoolboy. He must have been half Gil's size.

'Don't be a fool,' Gil said to him. I calculated the distance between him and me, planning to jump him and keep him busy long enough for Bruce to get away.

Bruce kept tapping the wrench. 'Did you know that I'm really good at sport?' he asked Gil, with such an innocent look on his face that I could almost believe he didn't know what was happening. 'I was first in my year at fencing and boxing.'

Gil lunged at him and I moved, tripping him up so that he fell at Bruce's feet. He grabbed at the boy's heels, but Bruce raised the wrench over his head and brought it down hard on Gil's shoulder. Gil cried out. I grabbed Bruce's free hand and pulled him away.

'Run!' I shouted. 'Run! He might have a gun!'

We ran. As we went around a jeep, we almost hit Tom, who was coming our way with several of his men, their sidearms drawn. Tom reached for me and threw an arm around Bruce.

'Thank God!' he said. 'Where is Gil?'

'At the bow. He hasn't followed us,' I said.

'Go to the wardroom. One of my men is on guard there. Don't leave.'

We went while Tom and his men ran past us.

But Gil was long gone when Tom reached the bow. Tom mobilized all forty-four of his men, and sent the seamen, except for a skeleton crew, to their quarters. The master and Popeye stood on the bridge deck, binoculars to their eyes, sweeping the deck. Tom and his men searched the ship for hours. There were so many places a man could hide. Countless parked vehicles, utility closets, the 'tween deck.

In the meantime, Bruce and I drank cocoa and ate sugar cookies in the wardroom, where all the casual passengers had been sent for safety's sake. We told them our story. Ronan sat in silence, brooding. I managed to tell my part of the tale without including how Gil bribed Roman. It would have humiliated him so.

It was late afternoon, after we had played countless games of gin rummy and checkers, when Tom and the master came into the wardroom.

'We can't find him,' Tom said.

'But where could he be?' Olive asked. 'Are we in danger?'

Tom glanced at the master, who folded his arms, his usual posture when speaking.

'After Ensign Bates finished his first search of the ship, he went back to the bow to begin the search again. One of his men thought to open a metal tool chest on deck. In it were Gil's heavy coat, his scarf and his life jacket. And there were clear marks on the rail where he'd climbed over it.'

'He jumped into the ocean?' Bruce said, his blue eyes wide. 'But it's so cold.'

I'd thought the same thing. Just thinking about plunging into the freezing water, full of drifting ice, was horrible.

'He killed himself, then,' Ronan said.

'Yes. I guess he preferred drowning to hanging,' Tom said.

When we went out on deck after breakfast the next morning, we saw land. It wasn't emerald, but Popeye insisted it was Ireland anyhow. By early afternoon we could see Londonderry and its port. It was hardly picturesque. The port was crowded with docks, cranes, ships of all kinds and warehouses. Like Halifax, only larger.

The *Evans'* launch collected Ronan to transport him to the port while we would continue on our way to Liverpool. We all shook hands with him. When Ronan grasped my hand he palmed something into mine. When no one was looking, I opened it and found Phoebe's ring. I slipped it

238

back onto my right ring finger. I hadn't regretted giving it to Ronan under the circumstances, but I was glad to have it back.

We watched Ronan clamber down the accommodation stairs with his only suitcase, much battered and tied shut with rope. We waved and shouted goodbye to him, but he only waved back once, settling into the launch and keeping his eyes trained on the shore.

'I bet,' Bruce said, 'that the first thing he does is buy some pipe tobacco.'

'Probably so,' I said. But I knew better. The first thing Ronan would do was find a priest and confess. After that would come the tobacco, a pint of Guinness and the bus home.

We were quiet at dinner. The absence of Ronan and Gil was a constant reminder of the tragedy we'd all experienced. That and the two patched holes in the exterior bulwark of the wardroom, where German projectiles had pierced the metal skin of the *Amelia Earhart* while we were cowering under tables.

We were lingering over our coffee when the master and Tom sat down with us. The master was in no mood for small talk. He looked me right in the eyes when he spoke.

'This is what we are going to do,' he said. 'When we arrive in Liverpool, I am not reporting any of this to the British authorities.'

Olive and I started to object, but he raised his hand to stop us. 'I'm not finished yet. I'll write a complete detailed report of what happened here, beginning with Eddie Bryant's death and

239

concluding when Gil went overboard. I'll submit it both to the US Maritime Commission and the FBI. Ensign Bates will convey the information about the defective tires to the RAF and the USAAF. There is no reason to bring the British into this. I won't have a bunch of constables crawling all over the ship and questioning us while we're trying to unload our cargo and get to dry dock. There are ships stacked up behind us that will need our berth as soon as we can vacate it.' He paused for a moment. 'And you all,' he continued, focusing his gaze on Olive and me, 'will not speak of this to anyone.'

I could see the wisdom in what the master said. We were an American ship, the murders took place in international waters, and the murderer was dead. I didn't much want to be delayed once we reached port either.

'Got it?' he said. We all murmured our agreement.

'I thought you might want to see this,' Tom said. He took a small pistol out of his pocket and laid it on the table. 'The chief steward found it when he was packing up Gil's things.'

It was a handsome object that had been well cared for. I picked it up. The bone handle was cracked. Where it had come into contact with Grace's head? I gave the gun back to Tom. 'What are you going to do with it?' I asked.

'Send it back to his family with his other things,' Tom said. 'It's a family heirloom.'

'Now,' the master said, looking straight at Bruce, 'don't you have something to say to us, young man?'

240

'What?' Bruce said innocently. 'I don't know what you mean.'

'We're now close enough to shore that we're receiving some routine radio transmissions, like the one we got this afternoon, from the British Foreign Office, inquiring if the Honorable Bruce Beauchamp was on board. It appears that this young member of the British aristocracy, who has four names by the way – Alfred Arthur Bruce something – ran away from his American cousin's home and is believed to be trying to make his way back to his family in England.'

'Bruce!' Blanche said. 'You're posh!'

Bruce sighed heavily, as though he was confessing to something unsavory.

'Yes,' he said. 'My grandfather is Lord Henry Beauchamp.'

'He wasn't a don at Cambridge?' I asked.

'Yes, he was,' he said. 'You can be both a don and an earl.'

'Do you live in a castle?' Alida asked.

'I suppose you could call it that, but it's a bloody ugly stone pile. I like the house in town better. It's warmer. But it's not safe right now.'

'Your grandmother will meet you when we dock tomorrow,' the master said. 'You will be there. Understand? Your family has been worried sick about you.'

'Yes, sir,' Bruce said. 'I hope it's just Grandmother who meets me. If Grandfather comes too, I'll be in for it.'

Olive, Blanche and I took a final walk around the ship that night, arm and arm, wending our way around the vehicles that would carry our troops into war on the European continent. Blanche was still reserved but clearly had a huge burden lifted from her. Olive and I realized that we couldn't exchange addresses, since neither of us knew where we'd be living, but Blanche gave us hers. We'd send our addresses to her and she would put us in touch. There was even some talk of getting together again.

We ran into Nigel stowing away gear in a locker and we gathered around him. He looked embarrassed, as a young man might be when surrounded by chattering matronly women.

'What's going to happen to you, Nigel?' I asked.

'The master isn't going to report me,' he said. 'So I'm not going to prison.'

'What will you do?' Blanche asked.

Nigel looked at Olive.

'I'm sure I can get Nigel a job,' Olive said, 'at whatever hospital I'm stationed at.'

'She's going to give me a reference,' Nigel said.

'I'll give you one too,' Blanche said.

'Thanks,' he said. 'Now I just have to figure out what to do with the rest of my life, without Grace.'

I'd forgotten I could look like this. My hair was clean, shiny and styled. I'd exchanged the glasses I'd ruined in the salt spray for my spare pair. I wore a wool suit and matching pumps I'd saved to wear when I arrived. My last pair of hose was free of ladders. Every other article of my clothing packed in my suitcase was filthy. Filthy from salt

242

and grime because I couldn't wash them properly in the bathtub. I couldn't wait to unpack the clean clothes packed in my trunk that had been banished to the hold for the entire trip.

I'd been told a car would come for me later in the afternoon, so I watched everyone else leave. The Smits carted their luggage down the stairs where they were greeted by a dozen or so fellow Dutchmen, who hugged and kissed them, chattered in Dutch and escorted them down the dock.

Bruce refused to let any of us kiss him goodbye, but when he saw his grandmother on the dock, he charged down the stairs and into her arms. She wore a fur coat and a diamond bracelet that gleamed even from a distance, but she hugged the boy fiercely. A chauffeur was with her. He tipped his hat to Bruce, who then shook his hand. Of course, Bruce had no luggage at all and still wore clothing from the bosun's store. The two of them, grandmother and grandson, climbed into a waiting Bentley.

Blanche left alone, striding confidently down the dock, turning and waving before she went around the corner to the bus stop. Olive and I shed a few tears, but we weren't unhappy; we were sure we'd see each other again. She was met by an army officer who took her case and led her to an army staff car flying red-cross flags.

Then it was my turn. I saw a man in an American Army uniform standing on the dock holding a sheet of paper, looking up at the ship uncertainly. I raised my hand to him, adjusted my coat, the one Grace had cleaned for me, tipped my beret and picked up my case.

'I'm Louise Pearlie,' I said, shaking his hand when I reached the dock.

'My name is Staff Sergeant Fretz, ma'am. I'll be driving you to London.'

'Tonight?' I said, surprised.

'Not all the way. We'll spend the night at Brampton and then finish the trip tomorrow. Have you got any more luggage?'

'Yes,' I said, pointing to my trunk that had been delivered to the foot of the stairs. 'I can carry my suitcase myself.'

He led me to the end of the dock where I saw a staff car similar to the one that had picked up Olive.

'And, ma'am,' the sergeant said, 'another passenger is traveling with us.'

I saw him leaning up against the car with his hands in his pockets. He looked younger without the beard and glasses that had been part of his cover in Washington, handsome in a sharp tweed overcoat and fedora. But I'd know him anywhere.

It was Joe.

Author's Note

Mary Jane Mulford Barnes 1913–1987

Mary Jane Mulford Barnes was born in a mining town in the Black Hills of South Dakota in 1913. Her mother, Linna Mulford, moved west from Jamestown, New York to teach school, married a mining engineer, and then divorced him before Mary Jane was born. When Mary Jane was six, she and her mother moved to Washington, DC for Linna to become one of the first women to work for the brand new Internal Revenue Service. Mary Jane graduated from Duke University's Women's College in 1935 in one of the earliest classes of the Women's College.

Mary Jane was always eager for adventure and, although she had trained as a teacher, she took administrative jobs in the federal government in the 1930s, so she could regularly quit and go on months-long trips. She sought a job at the OSS shortly after it began, looking for a challenge. She applied for transfer to London, never thinking she would be accepted. She had one month to prepare to board ship and sail across the Atlantic. Within two months of arriving in London, Mary Jane met the love of her life, another OSS member, James Barnes. He told her four months later, before shipping off for North Africa and Italy, that he would come back and marry her.

245

She gave him one of her favorite earrings to bring back to her (she feared she would never see it again) and he named one of his spy stations Maria Giovanni.

Mary Jane and Jim married after the war at Duke Chapel, moved to his hometown in Wisconsin, and later settled in Athens, Georgia where he taught geography at the University of Georgia and she ran the household and volunteered with Girl Scouts, PTAs, and many other groups. They raised two daughters there. She died in 1987 in California.